TEMPTED BY MR. WRONG

Dedication

I have so many people I'd like to thank.

First, and foremost my husband, Robert John. Without you I wouldn't have had the courage to pursue my dreams.

My mom, who has always been my guiding light.

To my daughter, Brandy, who teaches me every day to reach for the stars.

To my critique buddies, you know who you are. Without you pushing me to better myself, this book might never have happened.

And to Kim Killion and Jennifer Jakes, for the beautiful cover I'm so proud of, thank you.

Jacquie Biggar

What Readers Are Saying

Twilight's Encore

"What a captivating story. Twilight's Encore is the third book
of Wounded Hearts series. This is Ty's and Katy's story, i have
to say what a beautiful story!!!"
Nicole- Reading Alley

"THE REBEL'S REDEMPTION (Wounded Hearts, #2) by Jacquie Biggar had me reading this romantic suspense well past my bedtime. The characters are so well written they could walk right off the page!"

Avonna-The Romance Reviews

The Guardian

"Who wouldn't want to be swept off her feet by a movie star? And championed by a guardian angel? Sign me up! And like any great start to a series, the ending left me reaching for the next book. Highly recommended."

Christine Hart

Chapter One

Tammy-Jo Hawthorne limped down the side of the highway, broken shoe in hand, and cursed everything from the gravel cutting into her bare foot, to the drizzling rain making her mascara run. But most of all, she cursed fate for ever introducing her to her no-good, dirty, rotten scumbag of an ex-husband—Timothy Hawthorne the third, and don't you forget it.

Her cheeks flamed again even as goosebumps of embarrassed anger chased themselves over her flesh. They'd escorted her out; she still couldn't believe it. Not one person had stood to defend her either. Ten years she'd belonged to that stupid high-falutin club,

and no one had supported her in her time of need.
Well, screw them.

A semi-trailer flew past, and a sheet of water
drenched her to the bone.

"Ooh." She raised her shoe in the air and shook it
at the fading taillights. "Thanks for nothing."

Disheartened, she dropped her Louboutin in the
grass, careful to keep it off the scratchy gravel, and
wrung out the hem of her shirt. Tim had a lot to
answer for; not least of which was the fact her Jaguar
had been towed away while she'd been inside the
country club. It was becoming clear that this had been
a well-choreographed plan on his part. He'd thought
of everything too. When she'd tried to call for a cab,
she found her phone had been cut off. She'd stomped
over to a nearby gas station to use the payphone, and
found her bank and credit cards had been cancelled as
well. He'd taken her love and stomped it beneath his
wingtips and now he wanted her pride too.

Well, he couldn't have it, damn him.

If she had to walk the entire twenty miles to home,
she would.

And then she was going to sue that bastard for every red cent he owned.

The traffic snaked by in a never-ending ribbon of color, the noise a match to the static in her head. She thought about doing like she'd seen on television and lift her thumb to catch a ride, but fear held her back. Those were the same shows where the unlucky traveler was never seen again. She didn't plan on giving her soon-to-be ex that easy of an out.

The rain was falling harder now, coating everything in sight with a silvery glow. If she wasn't so cold—a combination of nerves and early spring weather—it would be pretty. Okay, maybe that was a stretch. There was nothing remotely *pretty* about being stranded in the middle of nowheresville thanks to the man you'd promised to love and honor until death did you part. The last of which was looking tempting right now.

If only she knew a hitman.

A throaty engine gearing down set her heart to leap-frogging in her chest—he'd changed his mind and returned her car. She swung around, a relieved smile tipping her scowl upside down, but instead of her beautiful silver Jag, a black-as-sin Mustang idled behind her in the parking lane, its driving lights blinding her with their brightness.

Now her heart pounded for an entirely different reason. She glanced into the ditch, but the forest seemed impossibly far away and the traffic never even hesitated, unaware and uncaring that her life could be in danger.

T.J. shaded her eyes, but she couldn't see the driver. She clutched her handbag. It wasn't much, but the soft lambskin purse held the keys to her house and her car—once she got it back—her identification, all the odds and ends a woman deemed necessary, and the proof that her husband was the reason she was in this predicament. She wouldn't give it up without a fight.

She picked up the only weapon at her disposal, her shoe, and inched backward, dismayed when the car stalked after her. Panic overrode decorum and she turned to run, but the ditch was slippery with the mud and rain and she lost her footing, careening down the steep embankment with a little screech. She landed hard on her butt and sat there for a minute, stunned. How the mighty had fallen. The Hawthorne couple were the envy of Magnolia, South Carolina. Everyone wanted to be them, have the same kind of loving relationship they had. What a joke.

And it was all on her.

A car door opened and a few ominous seconds later, T.J. heard footsteps on the gravel meridian. Even through the rain and early evening light, her white shirt practically glowed a neon *here I am* signal to anyone looking. And of course, someone was. She hunched over, doing her best to become one with the mud, and prayed like she'd never prayed before. Not hard, since she'd never followed any religious beliefs, but she promised anyone who was listening that she'd change. Just don't let her die.

"Tammy-Jo Hawthorne?" scary stranger dude called down the hill, his voice filled with amused aggravation.

What did he have to be aggravated about? She was the one sitting in a cold, wet ditch while a stalker… well, stalked her.

"Go away," she yelled, fed up with men and life in general. She swiped at a clump of ooey-gooey crap clinging to her leg below the silk pencil skirt she'd no doubt have to throw in the trash after this episode. Just one more reason to shoot Tim.

"I was at the club today," he said, and the sympathy in his voice made her squirm. "I heard about your car, thought you could use a lift."

She threw back her head and let the rain wash over her face. The humiliations just kept coming. The moment he'd mentioned the club she'd known who her dubious savior was; her evil step-brother.

Jason McIntyre.

Chapter Two

Jason folded his arms and frowned at the woman having a meltdown in the ditch. Angry as he was, he couldn't help but feel sympathy for his sister. Step-sister. No relation, thank God. Otherwise he really would have needed counseling by now.

"You need a hand up?"

She glanced at him over her shoulder, but didn't say anything. He caught the sheen of what looked like tears mixing with the rain, and cursed. Maybe she had her trip to jail coming, but even Tammy-Jo didn't deserve that lowlife she'd married. When he'd been asked to work the case in a colossal Ponzi scheme involving hundreds of thousands of dollars, little did he know he would be investigating his own family. The only reason the brass hadn't pulled him off the case was because they were getting desperate. And so was he. If he didn't find something substantial soon, his mother was going to pay the price. Which was why he'd been sitting in that ridiculously overpriced country club sipping on a fifteen-dollar glass of soda water when his lovely step-sister got her hiney handed to her on a silver platter. It had been ten years since he'd laid eyes on her and he wished he could say the time had mellowed his attraction, but he'd only be lying.

"You here to gloat?" she said, her back stiff with a mix of pride and anger if he knew her at all—and he had once, very well.

He shook his head at her stubbornness. "Why does everything have to be a pissing contest with you?" The rain was chilly and he'd only been out in it for a few minutes, she must be frozen. "My car has a good heater, Tammy-Jo. Are you going to stay pouting in the mud, or do you want a ride?"

That got her moving.

She stood, teetered for a second on the steep embankment, then began her climb, affording him a tantalizing glimpse of the soaked front of her shirt gaping open as she grasped at the wet grass to haul herself up.

About halfway, she stopped and looked up to glare at him. "Aren't you going to help me?"

He grinned, enjoying the view. "Nah, looks like you have it under control." He patted his pants. "These are my good dress pants, I don't want to get them dirty if I don't have to."

"Ooh, men," she growled.

If she'd actually needed him, Jason would've been down in that ditch beside her in a heartbeat—and she knew it. Tammy-Jo had been born knowing how to wrap a male around her delicate little finger. It was one of the main reasons she was now being investigated as her husband's accomplice. Her history with men made it seem unlikely that one would pull the wool over her eyes. She was as smart as she was beautiful—a lethal combination.

She finally made it the last few feet and stood before him, her body tipped weirdly to the side. He glanced down and frowned. "Where's your shoe?"

She followed his gaze over her dirt-encrusted legs and wiggled her bare toes. "I heard mud packs are good for the skin." She held up her shoe, the heel obviously broken. "I paid a fortune for these," she wailed. "And now they... they're gone."

She couldn't have looked more woebegone if she tried. Her normally impeccable makeup had run from the rain and the tears, leaving black rivulets on her cheeks like some kind of goth chick. The golden-red hair she kept meticulous now hung in sodden lengths around her narrow shoulders and neck. Her clothes, which probably cost more than his monthly car payment, were filthy and clung to her body like a lover's hands.

Not that he was noticing.

"C'mon, let's get you warmed up." He turned and walked to the back of his car, leaving her to follow. He popped open the trunk with his remote, intending to hand her one of the safety blankets he carried just in case.

"I'm not riding in there," she said, looking at him like he was a serial killer.

He hadn't considered it until now. Tempting.

"Well, I'm not going to have you ruin my seats," he said, only half joking. This car was his baby. He'd gone all out for leather racing seats with the Cobra emblem stitched into the backrest.

She started to limp away. "I'll keep walking."

Damn, stubborn woman.

"I was kidding," he called. "I was just getting you a blanket. See?" He held it up, the silvery material crinkling in his hand.

She stopped walking, so that was something.

Her shoulders slumped, then she turned and retraced her path, head down. When she got to him, T.J. looked up and something painful moved in his chest. Defeat. He'd never seen Tammy-Jo with less than a bucket-full of attitude and enough sass to light up the dreariest of their parents' parties. There was no sign of that now.

She waited, looking so lost and alone he wanted to wrap himself around her, never mind the blanket. Acknowledging that was probably not a good idea— and would doubtless end up with him receiving a black eye for his trouble—Jason shook open the emergency blanket and swung it around her shoulders. He waited until she lifted chilled fingers to grasp the edges, then opened his passenger door and ushered her into the dry haven of his car.

T.J. grimaced as she slid onto the seat while attempting to keep the mud out.

"Don't worry about it," he said, tucking the sheet around her legs. "I get Sally here detailed regularly. They can handle a little dirt."

She gazed at him with big doe eyes. "You named your car?"

He grinned. "Well sure, doesn't everybody?"

Before she could come up with a wisecrack, he closed the door and strode around to the driver's side. A text came in and wiped the humor away as though it never existed.

You there to work, or flirt with the suspect?

Do your damn job!

Jason glanced around, but didn't see any sign they were being watched. Not that he'd expected to. The people he worked for brought a new meaning to undercover surveillance. They were ghosts when they wanted to be. Maybe he ought to ask for a change of assignment. Not that they would grant him his demand. They needed an inside edge on this case, and he was it, lucky him. Now, he just had to figure out how to juggle all the balls without getting hit in the head.

Chapter Three

The technician yanked the headphones off her head, grimacing as her hair tangled in the wires. She threw the headset down and frowned at the video surveillance showing the Mustang's taillights as it sped down the highway.

"He's going to screw this whole case up because of *her*," she muttered.

"No, he's not," Cam answered, looking up from his cell phone. "We won't let him." He nodded to the other occupant in the van. "Follow him, Steve. We don't want to lose them."

Steve grinned and tipped his Dodgers cap over his forehead before throwing the deceptively cumbersome vehicle into gear. "No fear of that, boss. Put on your seatbelts."

Dani hurried to comply, aware of her teammate's propensity for speed. "He's still hung up on her. It's as obvious as the hook on Dodger's nose."

Steve glanced back, and Dani grasped the control booth as the van swayed. "Hey, I resent that remark. This nose is a work of art."

"Yeah," Dani smirked. "Something a three-year-old could do with Play-Doh."

"Leave him alone, Martel." Cam barely looked up from his screen. "Pay attention to the road, Steve. The last thing we need is the local police breathing down our necks."

"Sorry, boss." Dodger about-faced and continued down the road at a more reasonable pace.

"Pretty sure I know where they're heading." Dani said, by way of an apology. "The princess will be after a change of clothes and her husband's blood. In that order."

Cam nodded. "You're probably right, but we can't take any chances. Someone is pulling the strings on this thing, and until we know who it is, everyone is a suspect. Even McIntyre."

Dani scowled. "You don't really believe that, do you? Jason is one of us. There's no way he'd get mixed up in some stupid Ponzi scheme, no matter how much money is involved."

Cam looked up, his gaze dark and unreadable in the dimness of the van. "How do you know it has anything to do with the money?"

There was a heavy silence after his words, nothing but the muted noise of passing cars and the water splashing beneath the tires.

Dani swallowed hard. It was bad enough her crush was unrequited, but for Cam to know too? Unbearable. She forced a laugh past a tight throat. "Hell, it's always about the money, boss. Isn't that what you taught us?"

She swung back to her console and pretended to look busy. "Anyway, it doesn't matter. Jason is just doing his job, and it's our duty to have his back. I can't believe you'd think he might be involved."

"Martel..." Cam hesitated, then sighed. "Look, Dani, we've all been under a lot of stress on this one. The brass has been riding our asses for results. Let's just sit back, take a breath, and figure this thing out, okay?"

Dani caught Dodger's concerned gaze in the rearview mirror, and stuck her chin in the air. She didn't need anyone's sympathy. Jason had never made her any promises. And besides, when they threw his scum-sucking, pension-stealing step-sister in jail, he'd be free of her insidious web.

"Sure, boss," she said. "Whatever you say."

***

Tammy-Jo turned the hot air vents in her direction and cringed inwardly at the sight of her dirty fingers on the shiny chrome fittings, but she was too cold to care. Everything ached, from her skinned knees and sore feet to the jaw clamped tight to hold back cries of hurt and rage. Her life had sunk lower than a potbelly pig scrounging in the dirt at feeding time.

How could Tim have done this to her? There'd never
been any love lost between them, but she thought
they'd gotten along well enough, considering theirs
was a marriage of convenience. She'd needed a way
out of an untenable situation and he needed her
family's name. A good match, as they say.

Until six months ago.

The driver's door opened and Jason slid behind the
wheel, bringing the scents of rain, leather, and
testosterone with him. The roomy vehicle suddenly
seemed cramped. T.J. angled her body against the
door, the rough emergency blanket crinkling with her
movement.

Jason halted, one hand resting on the gear shift and
an arm draped across the steering wheel. His electric
blue gaze pinned her to the corner, the dimple in his
cheek flirting with her under the glow of the
dashboard lights.

T.J.'s heart fluttered. "What?"

"You haven't changed," he said. "It's been how
long…?"

"Ten years," she snapped. "Ten very happy, very peaceful years." Great, now her nose was running. She sniffed and looked for a tissue, not that there was room for anything so mundane in his big boy's toy.

"What are you looking for?" he asked, amusement ripe in his tone.

"A tissue, do you mind?" Gah, this day was never going to end. Embarrassment on top of embarrassment.

His teeth flashed as he reached past her to open the cubby and pull out a travel pack of wipes, tossing them into her lap. "Will that work?"

"Thanks," she answered ungraciously, holding very still until he returned to his side of the car. "Can we go now? I'd like to get home and out of these wet clothes." The words no sooner tripped off her tongue, than T.J. wished she could pull them back. Instead, she made busy work with opening the tissues and swiping her nose, relieved she could finally feel her fingers again, even if they were tingling—little sparks igniting under the skin.

Then again, as Jason shifted the car into gear and the engine let out a growl of repressed power, maybe the electricity in the air had nothing to do with the cold.

Chapter Four

Jason drove toward Magnolia and tried, without success, to ignore the shivering woman in the passenger seat, though her presence filled his car. She looked older, more cynical. What happened to the bratty teenager with the world at her feet?

"So, how's dear old Dad?" he asked, not sure why he felt the need to poke the wound. He caught her glare and bounced it right back.

"He's fine, and quit calling him that," she snapped, her fingers wringing the lining out of the space blanket.

Score.

He signaled, shifted down, and roared past a line of cars like they were standing still. When he glanced over it was to see her braced against the door, her foot pegged to the floor. An unexpected twinge of guilt made him ease up on the throttle and slide back into the Grandpa lane.

"Sorry," he murmured. "I forgot."

"It doesn't matter," she answered. "It's no more than I expect from you. What are you doing back in Magnolia, Jason? I thought you said this town wasn't big enough for you and my daddy?"

Yep. He had. And he'd meant it too. If not for his mother they couldn't have paid him enough to take this case. But she needed him, whether she wanted to admit it or not. He glanced at T.J. and grimaced. They both did.

"Well, you know… I figured it was time to bury the hatchet." He flicked on the radio, changed stations from bluegrass to rock, and back to country before turning it off again. "It's been ten years. Don't you think it's time?"

"What I think doesn't matter." She shifted, her mud-splattered legs peeking from between the edges of the sheet, distracting as hell. "Your momma missed you fierce. I'm sure she'll be tickled pink that you're home."

The lights of the town blinked like a starry blanket laid out on the banks of the Cooper River. He could just make out the covered bridge that connected the west side of town to the east over one of the mighty river's many tributaries. It wasn't a large crossing, but when he'd been young it had seemed like an insurmountable chasm. Then Momma met Sam Millar and everything changed.

"And what about you, Tammy-Jo? Did you miss me, too?" His voice came out huskier than he would have liked. She'd occupied more of his fantasies than he could count. At the time their affair, however innocent, had seemed illicit. Wrong. She was his step-sister for crying out loud. He was older, should have known better. But it wasn't until her daddy gave him the ultimatum that he truly accepted what could never be. It hadn't done a damn thing to stop the dreams though.

They were entering town limits before she answered. "A lot of time's passed, Jason. I'm not that love-struck girl anymore. Turn right at the next intersection." She pointed toward a two-story Tudor standing on a knoll set back from the residential street. A stone and wrought iron fence guarded the boundaries of the large lot. The house was ablaze, light shining from every room like beacons in the dark.

Jason glanced her way and caught the worried frown as she chewed on her lower lip. He had the insane urge to kiss it better.

Enough of that, moron. You're here to do a job.

"Looks like you have company," he murmured, slowing in front of a set of impressive black gates.

"Hmm?" Her attention was fixed on the front door and he noticed she was plucking the hem of his blanket. Something was definitely wrong in paradise.

"You want to tell me what's going on?" he asked, shutting off the car and dousing his headlights.

T.J. startled, as though she'd forgotten he was there. "What? Nothing is going on." She gave a nervous laugh and dug through her less-than pristine bag. "I was just hoping I didn't forget my keys at the…club." She hesitated, then gazed at him defiantly, daring him to bring up the afternoon's incident.

"Sure, darlin', whatever lets you sleep at night. Is there a way to trigger this gate, or am I going to get the pleasure of watching you scale the fence?"

She stuck her snooty little nose in the air. "I'm fine now, you may leave. It's been… interesting seeing you again. Thank you for the ride." She opened the door and stuck one shapely leg—shoeless—outside. "I mean it, Jason, thank you." Her golden-brown eyes looked at him filled with undercurrents he couldn't hope to wade through. She leaned over and bussed his cheek leaving him indelibly marked, then climbed out of the car and unwrapped that delectable figure from the blanket. Her clothes clung, revealing more than they hid and his body responded, as caught up in her aura as he'd ever been.

He was so screwed.

"Keep it," he said when she tried to stuff it onto the floor. "You never know when you might need it again."

She flinched and stared at him with a hurt expression that morphed into temper—true Tammy-Jo style. "You haven't changed a bit, Jason McIntyre. Kind of funny considering…"

She slammed the Mustang's door—his turn to cringe—and stomp-limped to an entry gate he'd previously missed. A foolish mistake. And a warning; he better get his head in the game. She punched a code into a keypad and the door released, allowing her entry into the less than inviting yard.

Funny, while he'd always pictured her in a McMansion, he'd figured it to be a warm and welcoming colonial like the house she'd grown up in. Not this depressing monstrosity. Further proof, if he needed it, T.J. wasn't the girl he remembered. She was a woman in a shitload of trouble and he wasn't sure if he wanted to help her or spank her.

**

Tammy-Jo opened the gate and slipped through, her face turned away from the security camera Tim had installed when they bought the house. She should have clued in then that her husband had secrets. But she hadn't, and now she was paying the price.

Damn him.

She picked her way along the slate walkway leading up to the intimidating entrance, keeping a wary eye on the set of double oak doors. She didn't expect Tim to be home. At least until she could get cleaned up and put her game face back on. Her pride had taken a serious hit today. And when Daddy found out... well, he mustn't, that's all. Tim was going to fix this or she was going to the cops with what she knew. If he thought threats would work with her, he didn't know her at all.

The rain had slowed to a fine mist and an eerie fog drifted over the manicured lawns and hedges her husband was so anal about keeping trimmed. It was all about portraying the perfect image. The wealthy, successful, socially active couple; pillars of society. What a laugh. In truth, they could barely stand each other. She'd moved out of their bedroom only months after the wedding, the night he came home smelling of sex and cheap perfume. If she could, she would have divorced him then, but the air-tight pre-nup his lawyer had her sign stopped that. If she left, she'd be penniless, and while the money didn't matter to her, it did to her father.

So, she'd stayed.

Until Tim pulled this stunt. It was over, she couldn't take anymore. And she looked forward to telling him what a low-life scum-sucker he was too.

Jason's car started, and the twin funnels caused by the headlights aiming toward the front of the house reminded her of a stage set. Appropriate really. After all, the past three years had been nothing but an act.

She glanced back, but with the darkness and the mist it was impossible to see anything except a blur of his features.

Jason.

After all these years, why here? Why now? She didn't even know where he'd been; what he'd done for the last ten years. He'd taken care to avoid her and

Daddy on the few occasions he'd been in town. Just a quick fly-by to check on his mother and then he was gone, leaving little hiccups in the fabric of their world. Uncomfortable, but nothing a person couldn't get over.

Or so she kept telling herself.

Determination strengthened her spine. Men weren't worth the trouble they invariably brought with them. From now on, it was going to be just her and Daddy—he was the exception to the rule.

She searched for the break she knew was in the hedge, but the darkness made the task difficult. Then Jason's lights hit it as he reversed out of her driveway and she hurried forward, only to go crashing over a mound of something right on the path. She put out her hands to save her fall and grunted at the impact on her shoulders as she hit the ground, her body toppling over the lump.

What the…?

Her heart about jumped right on out of her chest. Tim was going to kill the gardeners. He hated when they left things undone before going home from work.

T.J. turned over and sat up, her legs still flopped over the pile of dirt. Why would they leave such a mess on the sidewalk? They'd had the same landscapers for years; they were usually more careful than this.

Aware of another set of aches to add to her growing list, she lifted her legs and came up onto her knees, then placed her hands on the pile with the intention of getting to her feet. And that's when she realized the mound she was leaning on wasn't dirt at all; it was human.

Chapter Five

Jason made sure Tammy-Jo was in her yard before he reversed out of the driveway. He had no urge to witness the scene that was bound to happen between her and her good-for-nothing husband. Not what his boss would want, but that's okay. Cam knew all about his history with the Millars.

He rolled down the window and took a last glance into the dark yard. It was too late to surprise his mom tonight. He might as well head over to the hotel, get some rest, and go see her first thing in the morning. T.J. was right about one thing, Momma didn't deserve the asshole she had for a son. When he'd left

Magnolia with his tail between his legs, he'd promised to come home regularly, but that hadn't happened. At first, he'd stayed away because of T.J. and her father, then it just became easier to make excuses, avoid the confrontations. But, he was home now and old Samuel would just have to accept it.

The blanket crumpled on the floor redirected his attention to the McMansion. She should be climbing the austere steps to the main doors soon. Then he would leave. It pained him to admit it, but his protective instinct was still in full force when it came to Tammy-Jo Millar-Hawthorne. The new name stuck in his craw. There'd been a time when she'd promised he was the only one for her. Obviously, she'd gotten over that notion real quick. Wish he could say the same. He'd had other women, he wasn't a monk, but none could compare to his T.J. She was like quicksand, lethal to his health and his sanity. Which is why he preferred to avoid her, and if not for her unscrupulous husband he would have been happy to keep the status quo for years to come.

His cell rang out the *Highway to Hell* tune and his
lips quirked. Maybe that was his problem, he needed
a different anthem to live by. A quick glance at the lit
screen told him all he needed to know. Cam had sunk
to a new low; he'd asked Dani to do his dirty work.

He hit the Bluetooth link on the steering wheel and
connected the call, his gaze once more going to the
distant staircase. "Hey, beautiful. Whatcha got for
me?"

There was a moment's hesitation, then her voice
came through the speakers crystal clear and just a wee
bit peeved. "Boss wants to know what's going down,
and ordered me to call. Apparently, he's gone mute."

Jason bit back his tart reply. It wouldn't do anyone
any favors if he and Cam kept butting heads. You'd
never know they'd been best friends at one time.

"Tell the boy wonder the hen's gone home to
roost." He shifted into first and eased a few feet down
the road, inexplicably reluctant to leave until he was
sure Tammy-Jo was safely inside her house. "I'm
ready for a hot shower and an extra-large meat-
lover's pizza, in that order. You coming over?"

Why he said that when he knew the reaction he'd get from both of the parties listening in, was anybody's guess. He put it down to match-making, though a case could be made for cruelty, as testified by Dani's soft sigh.

"That wasn't nice, Jason. Why do you have to rub our past in his face like that?"

He shrugged. "Maybe he needs to know what he's missing."

"It didn't help with you," she murmured.

True that.

It wasn't her fault their relationship had floundered, that was all on him. He'd tried to warn her he wasn't a good bet, but she'd stayed anyway. And to his lasting shame, he'd let her.

"Listen, I'm…" A scream rent the night, raising the hair on his arms. His heart jumped into his throat.

He threw the car into neutral, slammed on the emergency brake, and was out the door before the cries faded into the dank air.

"Jason," Dani yelled, her voice vibrating from the speaker attached to the door.

He glanced back long enough to shout, "Call for help." Then he turned and ran for the gate he'd seen T.J. use. He tugged on the latch, cursing a blue streak when the door didn't budge. No choice for it, he was going to have to scale the fence.

He checked the holstered Glock under his arm and took a running jump, grunting when his chest and knees connected with the rock forming the base of the wall. But he had a good grip on the iron and used it to pull himself up and over the fence, surprised he hadn't gotten zapped in the process. He dropped the five feet into the bushes on the other side, grimacing when his bum ankle gave way and he tumbled ass over teakettle, but none of that mattered. His only thought was to locate Tammy-Jo and find out what the hell that scream meant.

Everything was eerily quiet now, except for his own harsh breathing. He took a moment to get his bearings then started off at a limping crouch, his gun once more leading the way. Where was she? He could kick his own ass for not insisting on driving her up to her door. If anything had happened…

There—a break in the hedge—something stirred.

He released the safety on his Glock and took aim. "Stop right there. Drop your weapon and step into the light. You're surrounded." A little poetic license maybe, but if it got the job done... He searched but couldn't see any other movement and his gut tightened. "Where's Tammy-Jo? What have you done to her?"

"Jason, it's me." T.J. stepped forward, hands in the air, her face a ghostly blur in the darkness. "He... he's dead," she cried.

The relief that washed through his chest at seeing her beautiful, grubby face nearly dropped him to his knees. God, for a minute there, he'd wondered if he'd ever see her again. In that moment, his priorities changed. The case be damned, he needed to protect this woman.

He opened his arms. "Come 'ere, honey." He strode toward her and she flew into his hold, sobs shaking her body. "Hush now, I've got you. You're going to be okay. Shh, baby, you're breaking my heart here."

It took her a few moments to become coherent, then she pointed toward a dark shape near the hedge. "I—I tripped over tha...that and thought it was a pile of dirt, but it's not," she wailed.

The distant sound of sirens told Jason help was on the way. Cam would want him to reconnoiter the area before the feds arrived. And truthfully, he wanted to know if what he was beginning to suspect was right anyway.

"Listen, honey. Did you recognize the body?" She shook her head and gripped him tighter. "Help is on the way. I just need to go check and make sure there's nothing I can do for whoever that is over there. I'll be back." He loosened her grip. "Trust me, okay?"

Her eyes were as big and luminescent as the moon that had decided to peek out from behind the dark and heavy clouds. He leaned down and just barely brushed her lips with his, afraid to deepen the contact because then he'd never let go.

He squeezed her shoulder in reassurance, then picked his way over to the shroud. He crouched, and using the flashlight on his cell, shone it on the face of the deceased. His gut churned at the sight of the dark hole in the man's forehead. Nope, he was beyond help.

He glanced over his shoulder. Tammy-Jo stood where he'd left her, arms crossed over her stomach. Almost defensive-looking.

There was one thing he knew for sure; T.J. had just landed in a boatload of trouble.

Chapter Six

He hunched lower in the seat. Two cop cars and an ambulance raced past with lights blazing and sirens loud enough to split the eardrums.

"Is it done?"

The voice on the line made his hackles rise, and at the same time filled him with apprehension. "Of course. I told you I'd handle it."

"Don't get cocky with me, you can be replaced. Did you get my files?"

He broke out in a cold sweat. "He swore they were missing."

Malevolence lurked down the line. He rolled his window down and breathed the rain-washed air. "Give me some time, I'll find them."

"Two weeks. If I don't have my documents by then you better pick out your headstone."

The connection ended, leaving him staring at the blur of red and blues through his front windshield. His fingers curled around the steering wheel until they turned white.

***

Tammy-Jo stood out of the way, huddled into Jason's leather jacket, and watched the black and white film playing out before her eyes. It had to be a movie, right? There wasn't really a horde of police and emergency response crews trampling Tim's shrubs. The flashlight beams bouncing off men and trees and the body of her husband lying like a discarded sack on the wet ground was like something out of a murder mystery.

He'd hate that, getting dirt on his good power suit.

Tim took fastidiousness to a whole new level. It was normal for him to change two, sometimes three,

times a day. He couldn't stand having the slightest
crease in his clothes. She looked at his muddied form
and shuddered.

Tim was dead.

Jason had told her he'd been shot. Who would do
such a thing? Why? The shock kicked in and her teeth
began to chatter. She sank to the ground. What was
happening? Someone shone a flashlight right in her
eyes. She flinched as though from a physical blow.

Her life had imploded. She may have wished Tim
dead after the stunts he'd pulled, but she didn't mean
in the literal sense. A harsh laugh escaped, one that
turned into a sob, and then the tears started and she
couldn't shut them off. It was all too much. Horrible,
wrenching pain swept through the walls of her chest
and seemed to rip her ribs wide open. She wrapped
her arms to hold herself together and hung on,
rocking back and forth like a child seeking solace.

"Tammy-Jo, stop now. You're going to make
yourself sick."

Jason's voice penetrated the fog some minutes, or
maybe even hours, later. She lifted her aching head

and looked at him, dazed. He crouched before her,
empathy turning his eyes cobalt.

He gently tucked the lank hair hanging in her face
behind her ear. "C'mon, honey, let's get you
somewhere warm."

He stood and reached down to help her to her feet,
catching her against his body when she stumbled.
"Can you walk?"

Just then the coroner's van pulled into her
driveway.

How'd they get the gate open?

*Oh, God, they're taking him to the morgue. I need
to call his family.*

Daddy. The random thoughts flitted through her
head, poking at the migraine flirting behind her right
eye.

Then another horrifying consideration came to
mind. She froze and stared up at Jason, everything
inside of herself begging him to say no. "Do I have to
follow them? Identify his body?" There wasn't
enough Prozac in South Carolina to prepare her to
walk into a morgue.

Jason nodded to a couple of men and a young
woman taking notes from the sidelines. His mouth
was grim when he met her gaze. "Let's worry about
that tomorrow. Your husb… the victim isn't going
anywhere any time soon. They'll have to run tests and
such." He forced a smile. "We'll tackle that problem
when it gets here."

He tipped her chin and searched her eyes. "I'm
truly sorry for your loss, honey. What can I do?"

Hold me.

The thought was immediate, but she'd been
handling life on her own for a long while now. And
the last time she'd reached out to Jason McIntyre he'd
thrown her to the wolves. Nope, not going there
again. She just needed to recuperate, get her head on
straight, and then figure out how she was going to get
herself out of the mess Tim had left for her to clean
up.

Easy-peasey.

As Jason wrapped his arm around her and led her
away from the chaos surrounding her husband, T.J.
was swamped by guilt. Here she was wondering how

she was going to save her own hide as Tim rolled by on a stretcher, his handsome face covered with a stark white sheet. They'd been enemies for long enough it was impossible to grieve, but that didn't mean she didn't care. At one time, he'd seemed like the answer to a prayer; indeed, he'd saved her family from losing everything they owned. She owed him loyalty for that, if nothing else.

Jason handed her back into the passenger seat of his sports car. He wrapped the blanket she'd left on the floorboards—a lifetime ago—around her legs and crouched in the opening. "Stay here. I just need to talk to some friends and then I'll take you to your father's, okay?"

She glanced curiously at the people waiting for him near a utility van. "Sure, don't worry about me, I'm made of good southern stock." She tried to smile but it must have come out a tad lopsided because he just looked concerned. "Go. I don't need you to babysit me, I'm a big girl now," she snapped, suddenly tired of the entire situation.

If she was an ostrich she'd bury her head in the sand. His stare made her uncomfortable so she turned her head and closed her eyes, praying he'd leave and give her a moment to pull herself together.

Perversely, when the door closed and he walked away, she ached to call him back. His stride was long and sure, his back straight, shoulders wide, hair a little long, curling over the collar of his jacket. He'd always been a rebel though, in and out of trouble as a teen, a constant worry to his mother. Then she'd married T.J.'s dad and his rebelliousness became uncontrollable. That wild side was catnip for the girls. He'd never gone without a girlfriend that she could remember. And the geeky, shy girl she'd been had hated the jealousy she couldn't control.

Looked as though nothing had changed either.

The woman—pretty in a cheerleader type way—hurried forward and lifted on sneakered toes to wrap her arms around his neck and hang on tight. Jason hesitated, then returned the embrace. His chin rested on top of her head as he spoke to the other two men. Who were they? What did they have to do with Jason being in Magnolia? And, even more… how did they know he'd be here, at her house on the night her husband was murdered?

Chapter Seven

Jason scowled at Cam over the top of Dani's head. "What took you guys so long? I thought you were supposed to have my back?" If anything had happened to Tammy-Jo... He squeezed Dani a little harder, needing her support as a friend.

Dodger slapped his cap against a muscular thigh, his corkscrew curls—the bane of his existence—taking on a life of their own. "Take it easy, man. We got here as fast as we could."

"Don't worry about it, Steve. He's just pissed at the world, ain't that right, McIntyre?" Cam's gaze was cold as it passed over Dani and then him. "Must get tough remembering their names in the dark. You'll have to share your secret one day."

Dani froze, then swung out of Jason's grip. "That was a horrible thing to say, Cam. If you two are finished your pissing contest, do you think we can get back to work?" She shook her head, gave Jason a fleeting look and stomped over to the van. She opened the sliding side door, climbed in, and slammed it shut, rattling the windows with the force of her wrath.

Dodger shrugged. "I'll go check on her." He tugged the cap back down over his hair and sauntered to the vehicle.

Jason waited until he was gone before laying into his boss. "If you ever come out with such a sexist remark again, I'll report you. I don't give a rat's ass about myself, but that woman in there deserves your respect. Sir." He tagged on the moniker to goad more than anything else. And it hit its mark judging by the betraying tic near the man's eye. He had the whole iceman thing down to a fine art.

They faced off like two roosters fighting for the same hen; chests out, shoulders back, full of aggression. Then Jason saw the other man's hostility for what it was—jealousy. Cam had been bitten by the little green monster. The anger drained. He, more than anyone, should know how it felt when it came to forbidden love.

He also knew Cam wouldn't appreciate his advice. Better to stick with the case. He nodded toward the departing coroner's van. "It's Tim Hawthorne. Someone double-tapped him and left in a hurry. I wouldn't doubt we arrived just after it happened, so the good news is the perp didn't get a chance to go through the house. I'm guessing whoever it was drew Hawthorne outside, then offed him. We'll know more after the report is ready. That's where you come in," he grinned. "Ready to hobnob with the locals?"

Cam grunted. They both knew he was short on patience and tended to roll over anyone who got in his way. "This investigation is taking some strange turns. Why would our guy want to get rid of his right-hand man? It makes no sense."

"Unless Hawthorne double-crossed him? Don't forget our friend Tim owed a lot of people. Maybe he'd become more of a liability than he was worth."

Jason glanced over his shoulder at the pale blur of T.J.'s bent head. He needed to get her out of here. He'd used his badge earlier to gain her a break, and him some time to gather information, but his luck wouldn't last. The local police were going to demand jurisdiction, and unless they wanted to announce their presence to the target, he would have to let her go. Which made every protective instinct he had scream a silent *hell no.*

"There's another angle we need to consider," Cam said, his fingers gliding over the keypad of his cell. "According to this," he held up his phone, "there's been a lot of recent activity on the market. Overseas activity," he added. "The Asians are not happy with the loss of their investments. We're talking millions here. That would be enough for me to want to murder somebody, so it's not much of a stretch to assume they feel the same way. And where there's big Asian moguls, the Triad won't be far behind. I think your

girlfriend is swimming in shark-infested waters and
she's the bait."

Jason clenched his fists. "I say let's take the
asshole down before anyone else gets hurt."

"You know we can't do that," Cam said. "We
don't have enough to hold him. If we move too fast,
his lawyers will laugh us out of court."

The rain started again and he glanced up at the
roiling black clouds. "Better get her somewhere dry,
your sundowner doesn't like wet roads."

His attempt to lighten the tense atmosphere was
ignored. Jason wasn't in the mood to make jokes
when his family's lives could be in danger. "I'll play
the game by your rules for now, but you better hope
nothing happens to my mother or Tammy-Jo or I'll be
coming after you—feel me?"

Cam stiffened. "You threatening me, McIntyre?"

Jason spun on his heel and strode toward his car.
"It's not a threat," he said under his breath. "It's a
promise."

He tried to shake off his sour mood before
climbing into the 'stang, but T.J.'s worried expression
told him he'd failed.

"Who are those people?" she asked. "How did they
know where you were?"

Well, that was a million-dollar question, wasn't it?

"I, ah… I texted that I was dropping you off at
your house and would catch up to them later." He
started the car and got his first satisfaction of the
night when Dani refused to let Cam into the back of
the van. She opened the door just enough to push his
coat through the opening before she slammed it
closed again. Cam stood for a moment, shoulders
bowed, then shook his head and climbed into the front
passenger seat. The headlights came on and the
vehicle drove by, Cam sitting stiff and silent as
Dodger leaned over and gave Jason a wave. Then
they were gone and all was silent, or as silent as it
could be with a dozen investigators combing the
neighborhood.

"Ready to get out of here?" he asked, returning his attention to the bedraggled woman who never failed to twist him up in knots.

She clutched the dirty purse in her lap and looked at him with a blotchy face and red-rimmed eyes. "Yes," she said. "There's nothing left for me here."

If only she knew how true that was.

***

Tammy-Jo was dog-tired, sore, hungry, and in dire need of a shower, but she recognized when someone was holding something back from her. Jason was stonewalling, there was no doubt about it. The question was why? What was it about those people he didn't want her to know?

She caught herself scraping her palms against her thighs again and stopped, clenching them in her lap instead. Every time she thought about tripping over that mound and then touching it and realizing it was a body—her husband's body—her stomach pulled the whoopy-woo.

Her brain buzzed like a bumble bee, stumbling from one thought to another. The late night meetings;

she'd assumed Tim was having an affair. The angry phone calls. The book full of names, all in code, that she'd found in his jacket and taken. He'd been furious, colder than she'd ever seen him. He'd threatened to ruin her if she didn't hand it over, but she'd refused. What could he do? They were married, what was his was hers. The joke had been on her.

Or actually, on him. That was some punchline. Murder. A strangled laugh burst from her lips, startling both of them.

Jason gazed at her quizzically. "Glad to see you still have your wacky sense of humor. Mind sharing?"

She shook her head, still trying to reconcile the boy she used to know with the man he'd become. "Nothing to tell. If you could take me to my dad's, I'd appreciate it."

"Are you sure that's what you want to do?" he asked. "Come morning the police are going to want a statement from you."

"Well, since everything I own is in that house—" she waved at the yellow tape decorating the property. "I don't have a lot of choice."

"You could stay with me," he said, then hurried to add, "at the hotel. I'd get you a room. Of your own. Different floor if you prefer."

There was no way on God's green earth that she was going to admit her heart had hop-scotched with his words. Damn. She should be over him by now. At one time she would have done whatever he asked of her, but she wasn't that naïve girl anymore.

"Just take me to my dad's, Jason."

She needed to see her father for herself. Make sure he was okay, and not... well, like Tim. Because she had a bad feeling he was mixed up in whatever was going on here.

She just hoped she was wrong.

Chapter Eight

By the time they made it to the outskirts of
Magnolia where Tammy-Jo's father had built
something resembling a mausoleum, Jason had given
up the idea of a good night's sleep. Not that he would
have gotten much rest anyway with T.J. down the
hall. Ten years and he was still as hung up on her as
he'd ever been. Pathetic, considering she'd obviously
managed to get over him just fine.

He glanced at her as he pulled into the winding
driveway lined with cottonwoods. She looked done
in—poor kid. Her day had been for crap long before
she stumbled over her dead husband's body. When

he'd taken on this case, he'd known going in he'd
have to see her again, but he hadn't realized how
deeply it would affect him.

She was a woman now. Gone were the willowy,
hinting-at-what-was-to-come angles, replaced by a
selection of curves and valleys guaranteed to stop a
man in his tracks. Her hair had grown out, too. Back
in the day, she'd worn a cute page-boy that
highlighted her fine features and big eyes. Now it
hung between her shoulder blades, the color of the
sun just before it set. He ached to see it spread across
a snowy white pillow—or his thighs.

Thoughts like those were not going to help his
situation. Tammy-Jo Hawthorne was F-O-L—
Forever-Off-Limits.

"Looks like they're still awake," she murmured.

Yep, it did. Which meant he was going to have to
quit thinking about sex and T.J. and focus on the job.
The next few moments would decide whether he'd be
staying for a while, or heading back to D.C. with his
tail between his legs. And yeah, that analogy said it
all. The last time he'd seen T.J.'s dad it had involved

a good beating and then he'd been sent packing. Jason let the other man get away with it then because he'd deserved it—he wouldn't let it happen again.

"Time to greet the puppet master," he said under his breath.

She looked at him. "Why do you always have to go on the defensive around my dad? He's never done anything to make you feel unwanted, has he?"

How long a list did she want?

Jason shrugged. "Not in so many words."

He shut off the car and stared up at the house. "How long did it take you?"

"To do what?" she asked.

He met her puzzled gaze. "To forget me and marry Mr. Not-So-Perfect. Rumor has it you met the guy not long after graduation. That's funny, because we were together just before graduation."

She stiffened and her eyes flashed fire. "Not that it's any of your business, Jason McIntyre, but I knew Tim before I… dated you."

Dated?

Is that what they called a wild and tempestuous affair these days? Good to know where he had fit into her busy love life.

"Did you tell him about us?" He needed this information for the case—and for his peace of mind. He couldn't deny it had wounded his pride to hear about her wedding only months after their break-up. He'd still been wallowing in self-pity while she was setting up house with another man. There was a lesson to be learned there. Most likely something along the lines of *once a sucker*...

"Of course," she snapped. "Tim and I had no secrets." Her eyes narrowed, daring him to mention the big, dead, elephant in the room. Obviously, there were some things her darling hubby forgot to pass on, like the fact he was part of a multi-million dollar Ponzi scheme for one.

Much as he wanted to be the one to inform her of just how her dearly departed spouse had financed their lavish lifestyle his hands were tied. If he blew this case he might as well look for another job; in say, Siberia. This was his chance to show the bureau he could handle his temper and be a team player. He couldn't afford to screw it up. No matter how bad he ached to take down the son-of-a-bitch.

"Well, sugar, you and I are never going to agree on this topic, so why don't we go in and say hi to Mom and *Dad*."

"You can be a real jerk," she said, getting out and slamming the car door in his face.

Tell him something he didn't know.

He regretted his words as he followed her angry strides up the walk. It wasn't her fault her father hated him, and besides, the feeling was mutual.

"T.J.," he called. She glanced over her shoulder and he opened his mouth to apologize, but then the front door opened and he snapped it closed. Resentment, a decade in the making, rose for the grandfatherly man standing in the opening like a benevolent Santa Claus. He'd fooled Jason once—never again.

"Daddy," Tammy-Jo cried, running into her father's open arms.

As they closed around her Jason was reminded of a boa capturing its prey just before it swallowed it whole. Sam Millar stared at him over his daughter's golden-red head. There was cynicism and contempt, but no sign of suspicion. So far, his cover seemed to be holding.

"Samuel." He greeted the older man, using his first name though he'd been told multiple times to call him *Dad*.

N.O.T.

Happening.

Ever.

"What are you doing here, boy?" Millar growled. T.J. jerked her head up and he switched faces, immediately taking on a benign, caring look. "Your mother will be over the moon."

"Jason brought me home after the most dreadful thing happened. Daddy, Tim's dead. Someone killed him right in our front yard." The words tumbled over themselves, her voice quivering with remembered horror. "Who would do such a thing?"

Samuel glanced at him then patted her shoulder. "Calm yourself, honey, you're babbling. Slow down and tell me everything."

A dark head peered around the door-jamb. "Sam, what's going on? Who's here?" A much-loved face caught a glimpse of Jason standing on the path and let out a joyous cry. She shuffled a couple steps, her gait uneven. "Oh, my goodness. Is that really you, son?"

Pain, helplessness, love, and guilt ping-ponged against the walls of his chest. His jaw clenched so hard it ached, then relaxed into a cocky grin. "It's me, Mama. Told you I'd be back one day."

He took the steps three at a time, brushed past the glowering older Millar, and picked his mom up to twirl her around the deck. "I missed you, Mom," he whispered into her sweet-smelling hair.

"Oh, Jason. I can't believe you're here." Tears wet his collar, leaving him feeling lower than a snake's belly. He'd called regularly, and even flown her down to D.C. a time or two, but with the progression of the dementia travel had become tiring and difficult for her. It had been two years since they'd seen each other face-to-face and he was stunned by how much she'd aged.

"You're still the prettiest girl in Magnolia," he said, setting his mom down and holding her elbows until she regained her balance. "How have you been feeling, Mom?" It was difficult keeping the concern dialed back, but he needed to know she was okay.

She shrugged, her topknot a little off-kilter. "You know me, it'll take more than some dratted disease to hold me down."

Yeah. He liked to think he'd received his bullheaded attitude from his momma. She'd been through more than her fair share of setbacks, but had weathered them all with grace and dignity.

"Come in, you must be tired," she said, peering up at him with clear blue-gray eyes. They'd always reminded him of a pearl he'd found once in an old trunk up in the attic of the house they'd rented—soft and luminous.

"He's not welcome."

"Daddy," T.J. gasped.

"Sam," his mom protested.

The only one not surprised was Jason. Some things never changed.

Chapter Nine

Tammy-Jo opened the door of the ensuite bathroom and a cloud of steam followed her into her childhood sanctuary. As a child, she'd loved the princess décor complete with French Provincial furniture, but now it made her feel as though she were stepping into a shrine. Her books—favorites such as Anne of Green Gables, National Velvet, and Misty of Chincoteague—still lined the shelves, and the thick, white carpet was seriously dated. She'd have to convince her father to give the room a face-lift.

If only that were her biggest problem.

She tightened the belt on her paisley robe, another leftover from her teenage years, and wandered over to gaze out the second-story window at the silver crescent of the moon. It had taken most of the night, but the weather was finally clearing. If only her life could change on the whim of the wind.

She was a widow.

The shock had worn off, leaving her at a loss. She should be feeling pain and sorrow, but after the events of the last few weeks the main emotion bubbling in her chest… she hesitated to even think the word— was relief. She was probably going to Hell for that. Maybe she'd even see Tim there.

God, she hoped not.

Her stomach rumbled, reminding her it had been hours since the luncheon fiasco. She could either ignore it and try to catch a couple of hours sleep, or she could sneak downstairs to the kitchen and make herself a snack. Hunger won.

T.J. opened her bedroom door and quietly glided down the hall to the staircase, grateful for the floor-to-ceiling window to light her way. The other three doors on this floor remained closed; one for her father and a connecting one for Caroline, and the one at the opposite end of the hall—Jason's.

She couldn't believe her normally sweet and caring father had spoken to Jason that way. If not for Caroline he would have left. She'd seen it in the angry flash of his eyes. Caroline had taken control of the situation, stepping between the sparring males.

"Enough," she'd said, hands out like she was a referee at a boxing match. "I don't know what this is about, but it's way too late to find a hotel room. And besides," she gazed at her husband with pleading eyes, "he's my son. Doesn't that mean anything to you?"

T.J.'s dad had stood there, his rotund body stiff until his wife laid a gentle hand on his chest. He'd sighed and given her a peck on the cheek, then moved aside for them to enter. "Forgive me, of course you must stay with us."

It wasn't the most gracious of invitations. Jason had hesitated and Tammy-Jo's heart had waited until he acknowledged the offer with a slight nod before it began to beat again. They'd entered the house in silence, Caroline leading the way, and agreed to meet in the morning to catch up.

How did one *catch up* from a murder?

The lower floor was dark, the closed curtains shedding little light. She ran nimble fingers along the wall, searching for the kitchen by touch, bypassing the switches. Good thing she hadn't lost her memory along with everything else; she made it to the kitchen with barely a sound.

Well, except for a slight umfph when she stubbed her toe on the bar stool set in front of the breakfast bar. Cursing, she limped to the fridge and opened one side of the French doors. Perfect, cold cuts and a kale salad. Just what the doctor ordered.

She grabbed a handful of ingredients, bread, mayo, pickles, turned to set them on the counter... and shrieked.

A dark shape detached itself from the wall and hurried forward to catch the items before they shattered.

"Are you *trying* to give me a heart attack?" she
snapped.

Jason grinned and eyed her from chest to lips and
back again. "I know CPR."

He really was incorrigible.

And too damn sexy for her peace of mind. She
took in the rumpled, just-climbed-out-of-bed hair—
stumbled over his shirtless torso, a tattoo of an eagle
taking flight from pec to shoulder—and followed the
golden-brown happy trail to the top of his unbuttoned
jeans.

Her own chest turned hot, her breasts full and
tender. Flustered, she tightened the belt on the
suddenly too short robe and turned to close the fridge,
immediately plunging them into darkness.

She let out an embarrassed laugh and hurried to
flick the switch for the under the counter lighting.
"Sorry about that." T.J. glanced at him still holding
her condiments, a quizzical smile on those swoon-
worthy lips, and waved toward the counter while
making busy work searching for plates and utensils.
"I'm hungry, are you hungry? I thought I'd sneak

down and make myself a sandwich. I could eat a horse right now," she said and stumbled to an awkward silence, abruptly aware of everything that led up to her being in this kitchen late at night with her once-upon-a-time lover.

Jason nodded and set the food down so he could open the bread and spread some slices out on the counter, calmly, with no fuss, as though he hung out with crazy knife-wielding—she set the utensil down—women every night of the week.

Maybe he did.

T.J. had no idea what he'd been doing for the past ten years. And she was curious. She'd often wondered what she'd say to him if she ever saw him again. *It was fun while it lasted. A goodbye would have been nice. Thanks for deserting me when I needed you the most.* Of course, she'd never say the last one, it would mean betraying her vulnerability and she'd learned her lesson on that score.

"Sure, I could eat," he said, his voice a low rumble so as not to wake their parents.

They fell into an easy rhythm, she buttered, he added the meat. She cut tomatoes, he layered lettuce and cheese, their shoulders occasionally bumping over the bread. It was just like the old days. Her wedding ring winked under the soft lights.

Except not.

Anxious to escape her thoughts she blurted out the first thing that came to mind. "When did you get the tattoo? I thought you were afraid of needles?"

He glanced down, then shrugged. "A few years back. Went drinking with some friends and woke up with a bandage and my chest on fire." His lips quirked. "I thought I'd been shot or something."

She flinched, imagining a world without him.

Jason misinterpreted her reaction and cursed. "Shit, I'm sorry. I'm a thoughtless prick."

Yeah, but not about this. He'd been kindness itself since finding her walking down that highway—was it only yesterday?

"Don't worry about it, I'm going to hear worse before this is over, I'm sure." T.J. forced herself to take a bite of her sandwich, though it tasted like sawdust. "I can't imagine why anyone would want to shoot Tim." She set the sandwich down, barely touched. "Do you think it was random?" Yeah, that made the most sense.

Relieved she'd come up with a plausible explanation, T.J. opened the fridge and took out a couple of soft drinks. She set them on the counter and popped the tab on her can, the pop, fizz loud in the otherwise quiet room. They needed to get back to bed soon. The thought brought on a host of images, each hotter than the last. She took a drink, enjoying the cold effervesce on her tongue. Better to leave memories like those in the past where they belonged.

Jason slowly lifted his drink and stared at her over the rim. "I'm not sure, but you better line up a lawyer to be on the safe side."

A lawyer?

Why did she need representation? Unless…

"You don't think *I* killed my husband, do you?"

Chapter Ten

Jason eyed the diminutive firebrand, fighting the urge to smile when the situation was anything but funny. Tammy-Jo had more spunk in her little finger than half the men in the SEC.

"No, I don't think you murdered your... Tim." He couldn't bring himself to say husband; it rubbed him the wrong way every time he thought about her married to another man. "But the authorities are going to look into your relationship, and when they do..."

"They're going to see a marriage in trouble," she finished. "I wonder if they have hair stylists in prison?"

She lifted herself onto one of the bar stools, her robe dangerously close to giving him a peep show—not that he'd mind.

"You're *not* going to jail, hence the lawyer idea. He'll be better able to guide you through the interviews than if you go it alone."

"But… I kind of thought you'd be there," she murmured, her eyes glued to the pop can.

Aw, shit.

This is when being undercover sucked. He tossed his sandwich onto the plate, a sour taste in his mouth and an ache in the region of his chest. Damn heartburn.

"Tammy-Jo, look at me." He waited until their gazes meshed. "There isn't much I wouldn't do for you, you have to know that," he started. "But my job… it won't allow me to be part of your investigation." He lifted her hand from where it lay clenched on the counter and ran his thumb lightly back and forth over the knuckles. "I promise I'll find out who's behind this and send the son-of-a-bitch to jail, okay?"

"Who are you, Jason? Who do you work for?" She
pulled away from his touch and leaned back on the
stool, shapely legs crossed at the knee and her bare
foot with tempting pink toes waving at him from
below. The woman didn't know how to keep shoes
on—it was damn distracting. And that robe…

"Isn't that the same robe you wore when we…?"

"No," she cut him off, tightening the sash and
making sure the edges were closed—which only
served to show full breasts highlighted by the swirls
of purple and gold in the silky material. "You must be
thinking of another woman." Her lips curled around
the vowels as though she'd tasted a lemon. But a
flush rose under the translucent skin of her neck.
Interesting.

"Darlin', when I'm looking at you, there are no
other women." He meant it too. Tammy-Jo lit up a
room with her personality. She always had.

She placed her elbows on the counter, the wide
sleeves sliding down to reveal slim, lightly tanned
arms, and cupped her chin in her hands. "Don't try
sweet-talking your way out of answering my

question, McIntyre. What are you doing in Magnolia and how did you just *happen* to be in the right place when I needed you? C'mon, spill."

She was so freaking cute sitting there, the under-counter lighting creating a warm, intimate glow that seemed to envelope them in a world of their own. Except he knew better. He glanced overhead. They were in the viper's den; it was just a matter of time before the fangs came out.

It would cause a rift between them if she knew the truth, so even though it went against the grain, he gave her the cover story and hoped like hell she'd forgive him later. "I'm a reporter. Those guys you met are my crew. We're in town for the regatta."

"That's next weekend in Charleston," she said, her gaze curious. "What made you become a reporter, of all things?"

She knew he'd been an introvert as a kid. Hard not to be when your father gets arrested for armed robbery and everyone looks at you like you're next.

Jason shrugged. "It paid the bills. And I look great on camera." He grinned, willing her to let it ride.

She snorted. "No ego left in your family, you got it all." She took another sip of her drink before setting the can down and running a finger through the condensation, leaving a roadmap that led to the ache between his thighs.

He shifted and redirected his gaze to her face, but that was no help either. She had a drop of soda on her lip and just as he looked up her little pink tongue poked out between pearly white teeth and licked the moisture away.

Jason growled.

T.J.'s eyes grew wide, startled. She stilled, obviously sensing danger. Smart girl.

Slowly, careful not to scare her into flight, he moved in, eyes narrowed on the pulse he could see fluttering wildly on the side of her neck. Everything within him zeroed in on the scent of her; flowery and sweet and something uniquely Tammy-Jo. He leaned down, over her body, and placed his mouth on that one tiny spot, her life-force. It jumped against his lips, causing little sparks to jolt through his body. God, she was potent. He used his teeth and nibbled on her neck, working his way up to her jawline, and then using his hand to hold her in place, he did what he'd been wanting to do ever since he saw her striding across that yacht club floor.

He kissed the girl.

Chapter Eleven

With the first touch of Jason's lips against her neck
Tammy-Jo whipped through a time capsule to when
he'd made a move very similar and changed their
lives forever. She moaned, the past and the present
colliding. She'd forgotten how good he could make
her feel. How the palm of his hand against her cheek
made her feel safe and cherished. How the teasing
little nips and kisses along her jaw made her ache.
She reached for his shoulders, needing to ground
herself in a world quickly spinning out of control.

Then he kissed her.

It was indescribable. Like a three-tier chocolate volcano cake—sweet and decadent on the outside, molten lava on the inside. She was pretty sure she melted into a gooey puddle right there on the bar stool.

How had she survived all this time without him?

She hadn't been given a choice.

The thought hit like a cold shower.

She pulled back, her hand shoving against his chest when he tried to follow. "Stop, Jason. We can't do this."

Thick, dark lashes any woman would kill for lifted over Mediterranean blue eyes. "I thought we were doing a damn fine job."

"Oh, you were," she agreed. "It's hard to hold myself back, but I'll try."

His brow lifted, taking in her less than lover-like attitude. He stepped back and took a long drink from his soda. Even the muscles in his throat were sexy, for crying-out-loud.

"Look, we've been down this road before. It's filled with potholes I don't have the energy to try and maneuver. Especially, since this is just a way for you to pass some time."

T.J. hopped down from her stool and headed for the door. Guilt for her part in what just happened made her stop and glance at him over her shoulder. "I'm glad you're home, even if it's not for long. We've missed you."

She hurried from the room, carrying the picture of his bare chest and inscrutable expression to bed with her.

***

Dumb bitch.

Her husband was barely cold and she was screwing somebody else. She should learn to close her blinds—he lowered the telephoto zoom lens to the windowsill of his nondescript car and considered what he'd seen.

He'd long ago learned snapshots equaled job security. One small mention of the evidence he carried and the money flowed. It also kept him alive. He always made clear if anything happened to him it would start a chain reaction none of his clients wanted.

The question was, what should he do with this information?

The boss would pay him handsomely, but on the other hand, he had a feeling the woman didn't know who she was playing tongue-tag with.

He felt like a master chess player, moving the pieces on the board to suit his purposes. If he stayed ahead of his opponents the game could turn into an interesting match.

Decision made, he started the car and drove away.

Chapter Twelve

Jason passed a restless night. He was tempted to kick his own ass for making a move on Tammy-Jo. She'd been right to shut him down, though his pride hadn't appreciated it at the time. He hadn't even been back twenty-four hours and he was losing his focus.

It had to stop.

He was here on probation. Headquarters could, and would, pull him if they caught any hint of impropriety. Lusting after his step-sister most definitely fell into that category.

This was his chance to prove himself after the fiasco in Cincinnati. And besides, his momma was

going to need him when the duplicitous bastard she'd
married went to jail where he belonged.

A muted ringing drove him over the side of the
bed to dig in his pants for his cell. Cam. Good, maybe
he had news. "Whatcha got for me?"

"Coffee. I'm outside, get out here so we can talk."

Cam wouldn't risk discovery unless it was
important. "Give me ten."

"Make it quick, McIntyre."

Jason flopped back on the pillow and stared at the
ceiling. He remembered his mom making batches of
pull taffy when he was a kid. She'd mix the
ingredients, set the pot on the old gas stove, and stir
and stir until it was ready. The air would be scented
with caramel, butter, and vanilla. Then came the fun
part. She let him help if he was careful and buttered
his fingers well. They'd twist and pull the candy until
it became a light golden brown, then cut it in pieces
and wrap them to keep their shape.

He felt like that candy now, pushed and pulled in
so many directions he was afraid he'd break under the
strain. His job meant the world to him. It proved

everyone who'd thought the poor McIntyre kid would go nowhere was wrong. But he wasn't sure he wanted to pay the price for that success anymore. Not if it meant losing his family.

He glanced at his watch and rose. Better get moving or Cam was liable to send Dani to the door. A quick shower later, he threw on a pair of jeans and a chambray shirt with a suit jacket to cover his handgun tucked in the back of his pants, and he was ready.

He opened his door and stepped out just as Samuel left his room further down the hall. Jason pulled up short, tempted to back up and slam the door in the other man's face. Instead, he had to pretend a friendliness he was far from feeling.

"Morning, sir," he said, keeping his tone civil with effort.

Millar felt no such compunction. "I was hoping you'd be gone."

So, the gloves were off.

Jason relaxed, leaning against the door jamb as though he had all the time in the world. "Nah, I thought I'd hang around for a while, *Dad*. Kick back here, in the lap of luxury. Sounds a mite better than some anonymous hotel room."

Sam's bushy salt and pepper brows caterpillared, his lips all but disappearing behind gleaming white teeth. "Careful, *son*. You don't have the womenfolk here to protect you this time."

It was going to be a pleasure arresting the old codger.

"You never have liked me, have you?" He hated the hint of little-boy-loneliness that crept into his voice.

Samuel stroked his goatee. "If it were up to me, you'd have been shipped off to some boarding school. Far away from Magnolia *and* my daughter."

He already knew he wasn't good enough for T.J. he didn't need it thrown in his face. "Don't worry, Sam, I know my place. I'm just here to see my mom for a couple of days and then I'll get out of your way. I'm sure you'll be busy anyway—now that your son-in-law is dead." He couldn't resist the urge to poke the tiger.

Sure enough, Millar bristled. "That's no business of yours, *McIntyre*."

The way he said Jason's name, as though he'd gotten dog shit on the bottom of his precious Ferragamos, brought a sardonic smile to Jason's lips.

"You're still the same supercilious prick I remember," he said.

He closed his bedroom door and headed for the stairs, aware that he was definitely running late now. "Tell Mom I'll see her at dinner." He could have made up some explanation of where he was going, but he had little doubt Millar would put his own spin on it anyway, so he may as well save his breath.

"As usual," the other man called out, "home for two minutes and you're off chasing trouble. You never will make anything of yourself, will you? Your mother must be so proud."

Jason froze, muscles tensing in reaction to the damning words. He should keep walking, he knew that. But...

He swung around and felt a savage satisfaction as Millar's eyes widened and he backed up a step.

"One of these days it's just going to be the two of us—no witnesses—and I'm going to shove my fist down your loud-mouthed throat so far you'll be eating through a tube. See how you like me then."

Now that he'd said his piece, the tension drained. He continued down the stairs, whistling as he went.

Maybe it was going to be a good day after all.

Chapter Thirteen

Cam tapped impatient fingers against his thigh and checked his watch for the third time. Dammit, what part of hurry up did McIntyre not understand? Five more minutes and they'd leave without him. The coroner was willing to talk to them ahead of the local feds, but only if they did it *now*.

He scowled at the imposing front door across the street one more time and headed for the van. It was only five a.m. but dawn was already breaking. Birds trilled their good morning songs, and a few early health nuts jogged by, giving him curious glances as they passed the news van. Probably wondering what juicy story was about to break in their neighborhood. They wouldn't be waiting long. Cam's team was making good progress; he hoped to have enough for a warrant in the next few days, though Hawthorne's death had come as a shock. No one expected the players in this Ponzi scheme to resort to violence. Though really, when you're talking millions of dollars there were bound to be some desperate people involved.

He gave a quick rap, then tugged on the side door, frowning when it slid open. "I told you to lock the doors." He climbed in and kept his body bent practically in half until he reached his chair on the far side.

"We did," Dodger said from the driver's seat. "I saw you coming."

"Don't matter," Cam answered. "Wait for my knock. We don't need to take any chances." He directed a look at Dani. "Any better?" Steve had warned him earlier that she'd been ill overnight. Not that she'd ever consider telling *him* that.

She glared at the back of Steve's head and shrugged. "I'm good."

Yeah, sure she was.

"Maybe you should take a couple of days off. You've been working non-stop for months now. It's bound to catch up to you sooner or later." He didn't like how pale she was, or the dark rings under her green eyes. She looked like one of those goth chicks he saw in the nightclubs back home.

She slammed the drawer to the electronics board closed, causing Dodger to jump in the front seat.

"Hey," he cried, rubbing the side of his head where it had smacked the window. "What the hell?"

"I said I'm fine," Dani growled, a look of desperation entering her pretty green eyes. "It's just a bug or something. I am *not* going to lie around in some boring hotel room while you guys solve the case and take all the credit. Forget it."

Cam straightened on the uncomfortable stool. He tried not to be offended by her words, it was just her illness talking, but still… "We would never have gotten near these guys without you, Danielle, and we

know it." Twin rosy red flags rose up her cheeks at
his use of her full name.

"Yeah, Dani, you're da'bomb." Steve gave his
ringing endorsement, the appreciation obvious in his
gaze.

She wadded up a piece of paper and threw it,
expertly hitting his pride and joy—his ball cap. He
grinned and picked the paper off the floor, lobbing it
back with unperturbed grace.

Cam hated the jealousy that rose with their easy
camaraderie. She got along with everyone else. Yet
with him, she remained stiff and formal. They'd been
working together for over three years now and it was
starting to irk him.

"If you two are done horsing around maybe we can
get going? Doctor Beaumont isn't going to wait all
day." He cringed as soon as the words left his lips. No
wonder he was on the outside looking in.

"What about Jason?" Dani asked, her gaze going
to the tinted window as though she could make him
appear by will alone.

And maybe she could, because in the next instant
McIntyre stepped out the door of his stepfather's
home and jogged down the stairs.

"Looks like he's saved by the bell," Cam said, then
added under his breath, "again."

Jason glanced up and down the street until he
caught sight of their van parked under a giant willow
tree. He gave a short nod and started down the road in
the other direction.

"Give him five and then circle the block," Cam
directed Steve.

"Sure thing, boss."

Cam kept his gaze focused out the window, but
that didn't stop him from smelling the citrus shampoo
Dani must have used during her shower. And that was
somewhere he was absolutely not going—at least not
until he was alone in his hotel room. As it was he'd
spent far too many hours fantasizing about her tight
little body in his bed. He needed to get over her. Find
a woman willing to come second to his job. Someone
to spend those lonely nights with, but not make
demands when he couldn't be there.

Maybe he should just get a dog.

"Okay, let's go. Keep a nice even speed. We don't want to draw attention."

"Me?" Steve asked, affronted. "I'm the epitome of decorum."

Lord, save him from idiots.

Chapter Fourteen

Jason pushed through the doors exiting the coroner's office, his stomach still doing cartwheels even though they'd spent the last hour in a conference room after viewing Hawthorne's body. Death was not kind to the human anatomy.

"Now what?" he asked Cam who was wearing his perpetual frown.

"We keep digging. I was hoping for a lead from the examination. She came up with nothing more conclusive than a close GSW to the head, suggesting Hawthorne recognized his attacker. Going by the lividity of the wound, he hadn't been there for long. How did you say you knew the doctor?"

As if Cam couldn't tell Samantha had been one of his ex-girlfriends. The Cap just wanted him to admit it in front of Dani. If the guy quit moping and actually asked her out, he might be surprised by the answer.

"We went to school together," was all he said.

"Well, it would have been nice if she handed us our killer on a plate, but since she wasn't able to get us an ID we'll have to keep working the pyramid angle and see who topples first."

"I don't like it." Dani turned and faced them, walking backward across the still quiet parking lot. "We're missing something, I can feel it."

Jason exchanged a raised eyebrow with Cam.

Dani huffed out an annoyed breath. "Call it what you will, but I've never been wrong, have I?" And when they didn't answer quick enough, "You know I'm right. You're just being bullheaded. If we keep wandering around blind, someone is going to get hur…yeow," she cried, stumbling over a pothole and almost going down if not for Cam's quick reflexes.

He grasped her arm, and tugged her straight. She
fell against his body.

They froze.

Jason wished he was wearing his Go-Pro camera;
their expressions were priceless. "You guys give love
a bad name," he teased.

Dani gave him a startled look, then jumped back,
narrowly avoiding the same hole. "Don't be
ridiculous. Cam's my boss." She turned and stomped
away. Again.

She was normally Miss Suzy Sunshine; something
was bothering her. Jason caught Cam's grim
expression as he watched her cross the parking lot.
"You going to ask her what's wrong?"

Cam looked at him with eyes that were unusually
vulnerable. "You heard her, man. She hates me."

Ah, no. "That's not true. She just sees you in one
light, you need to adjust the bulb. Wake her up to the
fact you're a man, not merely her boss." Just call him
the *Love Doctor*. Maybe he could look forward to a
career as a sex therapist if he was fired from this gig.
Sad truth was, if they didn't tighten the net around his

stepfather and anyone else involved in this scheme
soon, that might become a reality instead of a joke.

Cam shook his head. "Maybe she'll talk to Steve.
We need to focus on the case. How did it go with
your reunion last night?"

*Soft lips. Full breasts. The press of T.J.'s body
against his. Aching. Wanting. Letting go.*

"It went. My mom was over the moon." Too bad
Tammy-Jo didn't feel the same way.

"Do you think Millar bought it?" Cam massaged
his brow.

Jason shrugged. "Whether he did or not, he can't
prove anything. I just need to bide my time. He'll
screw up, and then we'll have him." And then he'd
leave Magnolia, and T.J., behind forever.

Cam started walking. "I think we should put a tail
on the widow. It strikes me as too convenient that the
moment we hit town her husband—who we knew to
be a principal player tasked with acquiring new
clients—is murdered, and the only other concrete link
we have leads back to her father, Samuel Millar." He
kicked a pebble and it went bouncing across the

concrete. "It wouldn't be the first time a woman was behind a scam of this magnitude."

Jason grabbed his arm and swung him around. "Get that thought out of your head. Tammy-Jo isn't like that."

"All women are like that if you let them," Cam scoffed. "Get your head out of the clouds, McIntyre." He shook free and his eyes took on a knowing gleam. "Oh, I get it. She's one hot little piece. Were you hoping to get into her pants, too? What's the matter? Did she turn you down?"

Jason's blood boiled. He lashed out, his fist landing a solid blow to the other man's cheek. Blood and spittle flew, splattering the road. Cam growled and came in low, using his shoulder as a battering ram that knocked Jason back several steps. Air escaped his lungs in a whoosh, sending black dots dancing before his eyes.

Dani and Steve yelled for them to stop, but they were too far away to interfere.

Adrenaline rushed through his veins, feeding months, hell years, of repressed anger and frustration.

Chapter Fifteen

Tammy-Jo woke late after a night spent tossing and turning—and regretting saying no to Jason. Those few moments in the kitchen had replayed in her head for hours. What did he think he was doing, crashing back into their lives and disrupting... everything?

A reporter.

She'd never have figured him for a social media person. He'd always been something of a loner as a teenager. She remembered all the girls totally crushing on him in school—her included. He'd been so different from the normal crowd, with his *keep away* vibe and worn clothes. T.J. hadn't told any of

her friends he was her new step-brother. She'd been
too embarrassed. And if the truth were told, jealous.
The special place she'd occupied in her father's life
changed. He brought a woman she didn't know, and
wasn't sure she liked, into their home.

And she brought a boy with her.

Seventeen to Tammy-Jo's sweet sixteen, he'd
made her young heart pound and secret places grow
warm and damp with just a glance from those
enigmatic blue eyes. She'd fallen headlong into her
first full-blown crush.

It had taken two long years to get Jason into her
bed, and only a few short hours to know she'd never
be the same again. They'd spent the summer learning
everything there was to know about each other—or so
she thought—and had planned to move in together
while she went to college and he got a job nearby.

When he suddenly left town without explanation,
she'd learned a broken heart does eventually mend. It
had taken a while, but she'd gone on to marry Tim
and become the society matron her daddy wanted,
and she hated.

Now Tim was dead and Jason had returned. Fate was a mean creature.

Even if she wanted to investigate Jason's intentions toward her, and Lord knows she did, there was no way she was going to pull him into the middle of the mess that was her life. He had a good career and friends, while she had…

She looked around the princess bedroom and her mud-splattered clothes from the night before scattered like ugly bruises on the white shag carpet. What if whoever shot Tim came after her? What if the police thought she had something to do with it, as Jason had suggested? Her first instinct was to go running to her father, but pride held her back. It was time she stood on her own two legs. She just hoped they didn't get cut off at the knee.

She glanced at the delicate gold watch on her wrist—a gift from Jason for her eighteenth birthday—and grimaced. Almost eleven a.m.; she was undoubtedly the last to rise. There were bound to be issues she would need to address, not least of which was an explanation of how she'd ended up the

laughing stock of the country club yesterday. T.J. had
no illusions about how her father would feel about his
precious daughter creating such a scene in front of his
friends and clients.

Not to mention the dead husband in her front yard.

She showered in record time, but then wasted half
an hour trying to find something in her closet that still
fit. The pants were too snug—she'd apparently grown
hips in the past ten years—and the tops threatened her
with indecent exposure. The dirty clothes on the floor
might have to do. She sighed and turned to step out of
the walk-in closet, then stopped when a ribbon of
color caught her eye.

The dress she'd worn the night she convinced
Jason to give their relationship a chance.

Could she?

It probably wouldn't even fit.

Jade green and made from the finest silk,
everything about the dress screamed seduction from
the form-fitting torso, to the sweetheart neckline that
showed just the right amount of décolletage to hold a
man's attention.

And it had. Jason hadn't taken his eyes off her the whole night. Her heart fluttered. This was crazy. It was only a dress. And she needed something to wear.

T.J. pulled the shimmery material off the hanger and over her head before she changed her mind. The cloth slid down her body like a lover's touch. She smoothed the fabric over her hips and gave a little twist, loving the flirty swish of the skirt just above her knees. Maybe this would give her the confidence boost she was going to need while giving her statement to the police today.

Poor Tim. There'd been no love lost between them, especially towards the end, and even though she'd wished him dead on more than one occasion, she hadn't meant it literally.

Suddenly, the papers she carried in her purse took on a much more sinister perspective. Could they have something to do with Tim's murder?

There was a ringing in her ears and her vision wavered in and out of focus. She put a trembling hand out to brace herself against the wall. Oh, God, what if this was her fault? Maybe, whoever it was had somehow found out the papers were missing, and killed him for it. That was it. Bone deep, she knew she was right.

Which meant she was in a world of trouble.

T.J. stumbled into the other room and searched the floor for her clutch. She was about to panic when she caught sight of it pushed under the edge of her bed. She dropped to her knees, almost hyperventilating, and threw the covers aside so she could grasp the purse. Her fingers shook so hard it was tough getting the clasp undone. But finally, finally she made it, and there they were, folded and hidden in the bottom under her make-up and wallet and glasses and various other odds and ends all women managed to carry in their bags.

She yanked them out, uncaring as her lipstick went rolling into the thick forest of carpet, or that her wallet tumbled from her lap to the floor. She turned and sank onto her bottom, back against the bed, and unfolded the five pages, dreading what she would find.

The first sheet contained some kind of complicated formula. It made no sense to her so she moved on to the next page. Names. Three columns. The first, a garbled—or maybe coded? —version of someone's name. The next held a date and monetary amount. The third? Another date with a total, but this one much higher than the first. What did it mean?

Tim was—had been—a corporate investor, so it made sense that he worked with numbers, but this was different. Secretive. It was written in his handwriting, instead of computer driven, and he'd hidden it away in the back of his safe—the one he thought she didn't know about.

The one she wished now she'd stayed out of.

Chapter Sixteen

Cam looked up at Jason with bleary eyes, wincing when Dani used the tail of her shirt to dab at his bloody lip. "I apologize. What I said about your girl was uncalled for, but the truth remains; if you can't keep your distance from her I'll have to pull you from the case. We clear?"

"Crystal," Jason gritted out through a clenched jaw. He knew Cam was right. His involvement with the Millar family already compromised their investigation. He should step aside, let someone else take his place, but he couldn't. His heart was here.

He offered his hand to Cam, guilt riding him hard at the sight of the red marks lining the other man's neck like a gruesome tattoo.

"Does it hurt much?" He nodded to the injury.

Cam grimaced. "Only when I swallow. Don't worry about it, shit happens. I deserved it. Let's move on." He chucked the frowning Dani under the chin. "That means you, too. We're a team. It's time we start acting like one."

"Rah, rah," Dani grumbled.

Steve handed Cam the cap he'd dusted off. "Let's get some breakfast. I don't know about you, but I'm starved."

"Ew," Dani said, turning green around the gills. "How can you eat after... that?" She nodded toward the low-slung brick building behind them. "That's sick."

Steve grinned and shrugged. "What's the matter, Martel? You pregnant, or something?"

Jason froze, his gaze as stunned as Cam's.

Dani gave them a *what's-your-problem* glare. "Does it look like I'm pregnant?" She jutted her concave belly in front of them. "Give me a break, you morons. Just because I have a shred of sensibility, unlike some idiots, whose names I shall not mention." She eyed all three of them with disgust. "You immediately jump to *the poor girl got herself knocked up*—is it contagious—scenario. Men are cretins."

"Well, yeah," Steve said, scratching his head under his Dodger cap. "If we weren't it would blow the whole evolution theory, wouldn't it?" Jason cuffed his raised arm, dislodging the cap. "Hey, watch the merchandise."

"You're not helping our case," Cam said, his gaze somber as he stared at Dani. "You sure you're okay?"

Her expression softened—*and wasn't that interesting?*

"I'm fine. Just need a good night's rest. We *all* do." She looked pointedly at Jason.

He held up his hands. "Don't look at me. I slept tight—*by myself.*"

"For a change," Steve added.

Jason ignored his friend. "I'm going to head back to the Millars. They should be awake by now." He didn't mention his run-in with Samuel.

"What's your plan if they ask why you were out so early?" Cam asked.

Jason remembered the joggers. "I'll just say I went for a run, needed to clear my head. They probably won't even ask."

He looked at Dani again, and made a silent vow to corner her later and find out what was going on. She'd lost weight she couldn't afford to give up. Her eyes seemed huge, giving her a waif-like appearance. If she was sick, he wanted to know about it. They were friends, and friends stuck together—no matter what.

Which led him back to T.J.

Kissing her last night had been the wrong thing to do, even if she was temptation personified. His irresponsibility could have ruined months of hard work.

It couldn't happen again.

"I don't think Tammy-Jo knows anything about her husband's or father's business dealings."

Dani opened her mouth, looked at him, then shut it and shook her head.

What?

He could absolutely look at the situation with an impartial eye. Too many details weren't adding up. Starting with the big *public* scene at the club.

"Seems to me, if the players in this little tennis match know they're running on borrowed time, the last thing they would want is to bring attention to themselves."

He looked to Cam for support. "T.J. was in real hot water at the country club yesterday. I saw it, and so did half of Magnolia. No doubt the other half heard about it before I even picked her up. And then there's the location of her dead husband. If she had something to do with it, number one, why leave the body in their front yard? Why not have it disposed of, along with any evidence we might find? Two, either she's one hell of an actress, or she was seriously shaken up when she found him. And three, if she's part of a multi-million dollar Ponzi scheme, why was she limping along the highway, in the rain, with no money, when I found her? I think we need to rule her out."

Cam rubbed his jaw where the bruise was forming. "I agree, it's not adding up—yet. But, we can't afford to cross anyone off our list of possible suspects until we have concrete proof." He stopped at the van and opened the door. "The only way to get your family clear of this mess is to take down the leader. The sooner we do that, the sooner your step-sister can get on with her life."

And you with yours. He might as well have said the words.

Chapter Seventeen

T.J. sat at the glass and chrome kitchen table stirring cream into her coffee and watching it swirl around the cup. She studiously ignored the probing looks from her father. Well, almost. She gave another tug to the bodice of the dress.

"You're home late today, Daddy," she said, hoping to dislodge his disapproving stare.

He clucked his tongue along the roof of his mouth—an annoying habit that had driven her nuts as a kid—and rattled the pages of the Magnolia Chronicle. "Seems as though I'll be more beneficial here."

He lifted the paper and displayed the front-page headline *Prominent Couple's Marriage Ends in Murder*. Her and Tim's opulent wedding picture glared from below, alongside one of the coroner's van pulling away from their home.

Admittedly, she hadn't been in any shape to notice her surroundings after tripping over her husband's dead body last night, but there were no reporters that she could recall.

Except Jason.

She remembered him explaining away the men who had somehow managed to locate him at her house, even though they knew nothing about her.

Or, maybe they did.

Maybe, she was the story Jason was chasing.

It was common knowledge her marriage had floundered. And since Tim and her father did business together, it had become fodder for the gossip columns. She couldn't believe Jason would use her that way, but then it wouldn't be the first time he'd betrayed her.

"I tried to tell you about Tim last night, remember?" She set the spoon down, then picked it up again. "I couldn't believe someone shot him. It was so horrible." She shuddered. "And then the police started asking me all these questions…"

Her father's eyes narrowed. He reached over and took the spoon from her grasp. "What questions? Why would they expect *you* to know anything?" He stared hard at her, the spoon rat-a-tat tapping over their picture in the paper, the drops of coffee causing it to smudge until their faces were unrecognizable.

Her arms and back erupted in goosebumps like little mountains of doom.

"Possibly because I was married to the man for the last eight years," she snapped, sick and tired of getting walked on by the men in her life.

He sat back, his belly straining the buttons of the white silk dress shirt under the pinstriped navy-blue tie she'd bought him for Father's Day. His suit jacket hung on the chair as though he'd been getting ready for work. She wished now he'd gone.

"There's no need to get your dander up with me, girl. I'm simply trying to understand how my partner ended up dead and my daughter became the main suspect."

What?

Her breathing faltered. Little spots floated in and out of her vision. She was going to pass out right there in her daddy's kitchen and he wouldn't be able to save her because he'd never taken the time to learn CPR.

"Put your head between your knees." A rough voice cut through the hysteria.

A hand pushed her face down until she was looking at the tile floor and a humungous pair of dirty, down-at-the-heel cowboy boots. Her dad wasn't going to like those on his spotless floor. She would have giggled except breathing seemed more important right now.

"Deep breaths. You'll be fine in a minute," Jason said from somewhere over her head. "You couldn't see your daughter was about to pass out?" he demanded of her father.

"She wasn't going to do any such thing. Tammy-Jo has always been something of a drama queen. You, of all people, should know that by now."

The sarcasm cut deep. Her dad never had much patience with her, but his condescending attitude stung. She'd always done her best to make him proud of her. Just because she had no interest in learning his business didn't mean she wasn't a benefit to the family.

She'd married Tim, hadn't she?

"What's going on? Why are you pushing that girl's head, Jason? I told you to get ready for school, didn't I?"

The pressure eased from her skull and T.J. straightened slowly, her vision clear, thank goodness. "It's me, Caroline, Tammy-Jo. It's good to see you." Jason's mom had stayed in her rooms the last few times she'd stopped by for a visit, so T.J. was shocked to see the effects caused by her early onset dementia. The once beautiful, vibrant woman who had stolen her father's heart was a mere shell of her former self.

"Caro, I told you to call when you wanted to come downstairs. I don't like you taking those stairs on your own," her husband said, coming to his feet and pulling out a chair.

Her fingers fluttered toward her graying hair, then twisted themselves into knots in front of her blue and white polka-dot day dress. "I'm sorry. I... I forgot. Please don't be angry." Teardrops sparkled from eyes as blue as her son's.

T.J.'s father scowled, but his hands were gentle as he led his wife to her chair. "I'm not angry, my dear. Only worried. I don't know what I'd do without you. Now sit here and I'll make you your morning tea, how does that sound?" He patted her shoulders and turned away to light the stove, but not before T.J. saw the heartbreak he tried to hide.

Poor Daddy.

"Hi, Momma, you look particularly beautiful this fine day." Jason leaned down and bussed his mom's cheek.

She giggled like a teenager, the years melting away. "Get away with you, son. You always did have a glib tongue. No wonder all the girls chase after you, calling at all hours of the night. I've told them a growing boy needs his rest, but it does no good."

So, she wasn't back to them yet.

Those sapphire blue eyes focused on her again. "You going to introduce me to your friend, son? Is she walking you to school?"

Jason's expression hardened to stone, but he smiled, his eyes begging her to go along with the farce. As if she would do anything else.

"That's Tammy-Jo Hawthorne, Momma. I've told you about her, remember? She's the one who helps me with my school work."

Well, that was true. She'd wanted him to fit in, just in case it got out that he was her step-brother, so she'd made an effort to ease his way into the curriculum at the private school they both attended. It was the start of her addiction. The more time she spent with Jason, the more she craved his attention.

"Your son is exaggerating, Mrs. Millar. He does fine all on his own."

Jason's eyes narrowed. Good. Her little dig hit home.

"Don't be ridiculous, your mother knows my daughter." Samuel said, coming back to the table to take Caroline's hand. "She doesn't *visit* as often as she should, but you must remember Tammy-Jo, don't you, darling?"

Caroline gazed nervously from T.J. to her father. "Of... of course. I just forgot for a moment, that's all." She gave T.J. a timid smile. "How are you, sweetheart?"

Jason cursed under his breath and strode over to the single cup coffee brewer near the farmhouse sink. His back was rigid beneath the blue chambray shirt. T.J. had to fight the urge to go to him and rub her hand over those tense muscles. Offer him sympathy and anything else he wanted, if she was being honest.

Warmth climbed her cheeks as she turned to his mother. "I'm fine, Mrs.... ma'am." She'd never found a comfortable way to address this woman who'd stepped into her mother's shoes. "I'd like to stay for a few days, spend time with you and Dad, if

that's all right?" And figure out where she was going
from here. It wasn't likely she'd get into her house
any time in the near future. And if there really was
someone looking for those papers she'd hidden in the
closet upstairs, she'd rather not be alone.

"Of course. We enjoy hosting. Don't we, Sam?"
Caroline clapped her hands, the smile she bestowed
on her husband radiant. "We must plan a dinner party.
It'll be so much fun. We used to entertain company
all the time, remember, Jason? I miss having people
over." Her smile dimmed. "Why don't we have
visitors anymore, Sam?"

T.J.'s tough, abrasive father stared at his wife with
a desperation that was hard to witness. "We can do
whatever you'd like, sweetheart. Just name it, and I'll
make it happen."

"Don't push. The specialists warned us to give her
space," Jason said, turning back to the table, a too-
delicate china cup steaming in his big hands.

Samuel glared. "If I want your advice on dealing
with *my* wife, I'll ask."

T.J. gasped, "Daddy."

Jason took a sip of coffee, his gaze on Caroline wringing her hands in her lap. "We're on the same side, Sam. At least in this matter, we are. I'm very grateful to you for making Momma happy. That's all I want, too." He sat on the upholstered chair next to her and placed his hand over hers. "Tell me, are you cooking for this fancy soirée of yours? You know how much I love your ribs, Mom."

The whistle blew on the tea kettle and T.J. rose to shut it off as Caroline smiled into her son's eyes. "Anything for you, my boy. Anything."

Crisis averted.

Chapter Eighteen

"I told you to handle the situation. It's all over the morning papers." The voice in his ear radiated anger and frustration. "I've worked too hard for this, Leo. Don't disappoint me."

The connection ended, leaving Leo with the tangy taste of fear in his mouth. He was dispensable, and knew it. Either he found the papers, and soon, or someone else would and he'd join Hawthorne in Hell.

If only that stupid bitch hadn't come home so soon. He'd been about to enter the house when she pulled up and then proceeded to scream the

neighborhood down. He'd barely managed to get
back to his car before the feds arrived.

The Hawthorne woman was the key. She was
bound to know where her asshole of a husband kept
his files.

All he had to do was convince her to talk.

**

The time Jason spent with his mother was
bittersweet. She remained the same sweet person
she'd always been, yet different. Her memory of the
past was sometimes embarrassingly accurate, and yet
basics like her love of sugar in her tea or Tammy-Jo's
name had disappeared into the mists of her mind.
How long before he too vanished from her thoughts?

It was a dismal outlook.

The disease stealing her away bit by bit didn't
care. It was a cruel monster that fed off her confusion
and grew stronger with every misplaced item or
forgotten taste.

If only they'd picked up on the signs sooner; found
some kind of treatment to give her more time. Sudden
mood swings and mislaid things, like the silverware

ending up in the fridge, was put down to aging—
absentmindedness. It wasn't until she overstocked the
cupboards with boxes of tissue, and then shredded
them, that Sam realized there was a problem. He'd
taken her to the best doctors money could buy, but to
no avail.

All they could do now was enjoy the time they had
left.

Which made the fact he'd been called upon to
investigate his step-father something of a double-
edged sword. If only...

The ting of an incoming message had everyone
scrambling for their phones. It was Sam's. He read
the note and his expression darkened. He pushed back
his chair and stood, glancing at T.J briefly before
bending to kiss Caroline's smooth cheek.

"I must take this call. We'll talk after I'm
through," he said to his daughter.

Caroline patted his shoulder. "Take your time,
dear." She smiled. "I'm looking forward to hearing
what these two have been getting up to, it's been so
long since we've had time to chat."

Jason almost laughed at the grim look leveled his way. What did Sam think he would say? "Hey, ma, did you know you're living with a criminal?" Somehow, he didn't think she'd appreciate hearing those words. As long as Sam did right by her, he was willing to live with the status quo—at least until they had a solid case against the man.

He couldn't forget they had a killer on the loose though.

He looked at Sam. "I think it's better if I hang around for a few days anyway. Make sure the women are cared for."

Tammy-Jo paled while Caroline looked puzzled. "Why on earth would you say such a thing, Jason? Sam spoils me rotten, and I'm sure Timothy does the same for T.J."

She was with them again.

T.J. gave him a desperate glance, then reached across the table to lift one of his mom's slender hands. "That's why I'm staying here for a while, Tim was… killed last night."

Caroline gasped, her gaze jumping from Sam to Jason and back to Tammy-Jo. "Killed? What do you mean, child? Was he in a car accident?" She leaned forward to pull T.J. into her arms. "You poor, poor girl."

Jason hesitated, reluctant to upset her any further. "Not an accident, Momma."

"Let it go," Sam warned.

Caroline released T.J. to search her husband's face. "Let what go? What happened?" She turned to Jason and frowned. "Tell me."

Jason's neck grew warm. He wished now he'd let it ride. "Tammy-Jo's husband was shot and killed outside their home, Mom. T.J. found him."

Her hand fluttered to her mouth. "Oh, no." Tears hovered on the ends of her lashes. "I can't imagine. No wonder you seemed so upset last night." She turned to Sam. "You knew about this, didn't you?"

His head snapped back like he'd been hit. "I appreciate you wanting to protect me, but she's my daughter too, Sam. I deserve to know."

Something like relief flashed in his eyes before he strode to his wife and leaned down to kiss her. "I love you," he said.

She smiled, though it was wobbly. "And I you. Please don't hide things from me anymore. There's so much I seem to forget already. I need to know I can count on you for the truth."

He nodded. "Trust me. I will never do anything to deliberately hurt you. I'd planned on telling you about Tim." He shot a glare at Jason. "I didn't get the chance." His phone buzzed again, the noise strident in the silence of the kitchen. "See you later?"

Caroline's expression was melancholy. "Of course."

As she watched her husband leave the room, Jason had the feeling there were issues between the couple that had nothing to do with her diagnosis.

"What are your plans for the day, Momma?" he asked, seeking to lighten her mood. "How about I take you out for a late lunch, my treat?"

She turned back to him, a faraway gleam in her eyes. "Hmm? Why, yes, that sounds lovely. But only if your girlfriend can join us." She smiled at T.J. "I enjoy meeting his friends."

Tammy-Jo answered without missing a beat. "He's told me so much about you, Mrs. Hawthorne. It's nice to finally meet you face to face."

She took a step in the direction her father had taken. "I'll just freshen up before we leave. Bathrooms are that way, I presume."

Jason gritted his teeth and nodded. He needed to know what those two were about to say to each other, but he couldn't very well leave his mother alone.

And Tammy-Jo knew that.

Well played.

Chapter Nineteen

T.J. followed her father down the hall to his office, aware of the eyes boring a hole in her back. She'd worry about Jason later. Right now she needed to know what she should do about the documents in her possession. Her first instinct was to turn them over to the police, but something held her back. If she was right and Tim had died because of those papers, they might be the only thing keeping her alive.

A mouse ran over her grave. She rubbed her arms to get rid of the ghostly shivers and straightened her spine. She wasn't dead yet, damn it, and didn't plan on getting there any time soon. If only she could trust

Jason, but he wasn't telling her everything and she couldn't afford to wait in the hope he'd come clean. It was too coincidental that he'd turned up just as her life imploded.

He *said* he was a journalist, but what if he was the one behind Tim's death?

No. Her heart rejected the idea even as her head acknowledged the possibility. He'd been in the right place, at the right time, and could have had the means. The question was why? What drove a man to murder?

Jealousy.

Even as her pulse thrilled at the thought, T.J. cast it aside. Jason had been the one to leave her, it wasn't likely he'd nourished an everlasting love and suddenly decided to get rid of the competition.

So, that left... money.

The root of all evil.

It made perfect sense. Jason had come from a dirt-poor childhood into a house filled with every luxury. She'd tried to help him fit in, but he'd carried a chip on his shoulder, and in the end, it destroyed their relationship.

But murder?

She just didn't know.

Her father entered the office, then turned to glance down the hall. She ducked into an alcove and narrowly missed bumping against a portrait of Caroline. Her heart pounded. Why was she hiding?

His voice carried through the opening, tired, angry. "What do you want? I gave you what you asked for… leave my family out of this." There was more, but she couldn't hear, then suddenly it was loud and clear. "Touch her and it's over. You hear me? I'll destroy you, you sonofabitch."

Something hit the floor and then he was there, ripping the door back on its hinges, his face an ugly purple-red with suppressed rage and… dread? What did her strong and powerful father have to fear?

"Daddy, what's wrong?' She pushed aside her own trepidation and stepped forward to lay a comforting hand on his arm. "Who was on the phone?"

He pulled away and paced across the room to the liquor cabinet, his strides stiff with the cold tension filling the room.

T.J. waged a silent war whether she should leave and come back later, or stay and poke the dragon. She dragged her feet entering the room and leaned against the closed door, but kept her hand on the knob. Immediately, the air seemed heavier, filled with undercurrents that did nothing to curb her anxiety.

Her dad turned, his eyes squinting as he took a healthy swallow of the amber liquid before raising his glass, "Care for a drink?"

She shook her head, repulsed. "It's barely noon. This isn't like you. Tell me what's going on, maybe I can help."

He ran a tired hand through still thick gray hair and rubbed the back of his neck. "It's nothing. A project I'm working on is giving me some grief, and now, with Tim…" He gulped the rest of the scotch down and refilled his glass. "I'll figure it out." He eyed her hand on the door knob. "Was there something you needed?"

T.J. tried not to feel rebuffed, but it was hard. Her father loved her, she'd never doubted that. Just as she'd never doubted he'd wished for a son. It fueled her love-hate relationship with Jason in the early days, until it became clear the two males in the household could barely stand one another. Then, she'd found herself championing the teenaged boy, not that he appreciated it, or her.

That came later.

Now that she was here, T.J. wasn't sure how to start. Her heels made click-click statements of their own as she crossed the hardwood floor and took a seat in one of the twin club chairs. Dragonflies decorated the shade of a lamp sitting on the end table, their cobalt blue eyes glowing. It made her nervous, that light.

They'd been close once, her and her dad.

She tried to hold onto that image as she told him about the breakdown of her marriage, the humiliation at the club, Jason's rescue, finding Tim dead on their lawn, and finally, the papers she felt sure caused his murder.

Each revelation helped to lift the oppressive weight she'd been carrying on her shoulders the last few months. When it was over, she sighed and sat back, her head pillowed by the tufted leather. It felt good to talk with someone she trusted. Tim had weaned her away from her friends without her even realizing until it was too late. He'd even found ways to keep her from her family. And she'd gone along with it, determined to be the good wife—if not the most loving.

"Why didn't you come to me sooner?" her father demanded, taking the other chair. It groaned beneath his bulk, the air whooshing out of the cushions like a pricked balloon. His goatee under the yellow glow of the lamp gave him a faintly satanic look.

She sat up and crossed, then uncrossed her legs, instead sticking one foot primly behind the other. "I thought I could handle it, Dad. Tim is… was, my problem, not yours."

He frowned. "You're still *my* daughter, young lady. Hawthorne was my partner, but you have my one hundred percent support. How could you ever doubt that?"

Maybe because the two men had bonded to the point she'd felt superfluous?

Even now, there was a distance between her and her father that had never existed before. One she was desperate to bridge.

She leaned over and grasped his hand, surprised by the cool, clammy feel of it. Actually, his face seemed pasty too. Her stomach dropped. She glared at the nearly empty tumbler in his other hand. "Are you feeling okay? It's not like you to drink like this."

His bushy brows lowered, giving him the appearance of a swooping hawk. "It's not every day I learn a man I'd trusted with my only daughter's hand in marriage not only hurt her, he swindled me.

"I'm glad the son-of-a-bitch is dead."

Chapter Twenty

Tammy-Jo stared at her father as if she'd never seen him before. This cold, vindictive person wasn't the man she'd grown up with. The kind-hearted, easy-to-laughter dad who'd let her ride horsey on his knee seemed like a figment of her imagination.

"Dad, you don't mean that." She looked around, anxious to ensure the door was still closed and no one had heard his words. It was bad enough the police were going to delve into her background in the search for Tim's killer, she didn't want her father to become a suspect.

He paced around the room. "Don't I? We were fine until that miscreant came into our lives. Look at us now. If not for him, you wouldn't have hurried into a relationship with Hawthorne and we could have avoided this whole sticky mess."

Shocked, T.J. realized he was talking about Jason.

"You've never given Jason a chance. He had it hard as a kid. Why did you hate him so much?"

He stopped and stared, as though surprised by the question. "Hatred's rather strong. How did you expect me to feel? I disliked his influence on you, and that was before he attempted to defile my baby girl."

His words startled a laugh out of her. "*Defile*? We aren't living in the seventeenth century, Daddy. I was sixteen, hardly a child. What happened between Jason and me was sweet and wonderful—until you turned it into a dirty secret. If anyone's at fault here, it's you." The conviction in her tone stunned her, but it was true. It had created a rift in their family. For a while, she'd worried it might even cause a separation between her father and Caroline, but they'd managed

It rose in a demonic cloud and kept him on his feet.
He shoved for all he was worth, using his hands to
heave the muscular shoulder away from his
diaphragm, and then up to wrap them around his
adversary's neck, squeezing until he felt the strength
leaving the guy's body. He kept his grip until his
fingers went numb and his arms shook from the
pressure.

Dazed, he took a shaky step back. Reality set in
when Dani fell to her knees beside the groggy man,
her gaze accusing as she looked up at him. "What the
hell were you thinking, Jason?"

Good question.

He rubbed his mouth, wincing at the ache in his
chest, and realized he'd probably just signed his
termination papers. How was he going to protect his
mother and Tammy-Jo now?

to work it out, though there was a strain between them that hadn't been there before.

"You can't keep blaming Jason, Dad. There were two of us in that bed. I'm the one who lured him into my room. I know you don't believe me, but it's the truth. And it's certainly not his fault that I married Tim." She cocked her head. "Why are you prevaricating? Who were you talking to on the phone earlier? It sounded serious."

He scrubbed a hand over his face and stared at her with sunken eyes, reminding her of a wizened old elf.

"A client. I told you, it's nothing to worry about." His gaze slid to the scotch on the table beside her. "Have you looked into getting a lawyer yet?"

She shook her head. "Jason said I would need one, but…"

Her dad stiffened. "What does *he* have to do with this? You've already asked his advice?"

Frustrated, T.J. rose and stalked toward the door. "No, I did not ask Jason for anything. As I mentioned last night, he happened to see my embarrassment at the country club and followed to make sure I was

okay." She frowned at her father's skeptical
expression. "He was just being nice, Dad. There's no
law against kindness, is there?" Sighing, she carried
on, "Anyway, he picked me up walking home since
Tim had my car towed. Jason offered me a ride and I
took it, I won't apologize for that. When we got to my
house, he dropped me off, and that's when I found
Tim lying dead on the ground.

"Jason said it's normal for the police to study
family and friends first before broadening their
investigation. I didn't want a lawyer, but he seems to
think it's the smart thing to do. *That's* why I followed
you in here; I was wondering if you could
recommend someone."

He nodded. "I'll talk to some people. How soon
before the *po*-lice show up at my door?"

T.J. cringed, well aware the *po*-lice, as her daddy
called them, wouldn't have reason to come a-callin' if
not for her. "I was planning on going down to the
station to give my statement. That way they'd have no
reason to bother you and Caroline." She voiced aloud
the horrible thoughts churning in her head and

making her stomach roil. "I'm sorry Tim is dead, but
I'm not grieving. Does that make me a bad person?"

Her father held out his arms and she flew into their
comforting warmth.

"It makes you human," he said, kissing her
forehead. "Now, let's have no more of this talk."

He stepped back and looked her in the eye, his
fingers wrapped around her upper arms. "You just
worry about keeping your story straight for the police,
and I'll handle the rest." He gave a reassuring squeeze
and released her, stepping away to pick up his drink.
"Bring me those papers you mentioned, will you?"
His hand shook, sloshing some of the drink onto his
shirt, leaving a dark stain like an exclamation mark
over his heart. "And keep it between the two of us
until I see what's in them, that's a good girl."

The dragonfly stared at him with opaque blue eyes.

Tammy-Jo gave a faint nod and opened the door,
suddenly desperate to escape. What did he mean?
He'd scared her. She'd received the impression he
was giving her a warning.

The question was; why?

***

Jason escorted his mom up to her room so she could get ready for their dinner date. Joy and guilt held hands in his heart as he walked downstairs. She'd been so excited by his invitation it filled him with pleasure, but also remorse for all the years he'd been away. He questioned the decisions he'd made the night he left Magnolia with his career in jeopardy and his mother's health floundering the way it was.

And then there was the torch he still carried for one stubborn, auburn-haired vixen. He rounded the corner and slowed. T.J. leaned, right shoulder against the wall and head bowed, a few feet from her father's office. He frowned. What had the jerk done now?

"Hey," he said, his voice soft so as not to startle her. "What's wrong?"

She looked up and he swore under his breath. She was upset, her eyes too big in her narrow face. He closed the space between them and lifted a gentle hand to her jaw. "Talk to me, honey. What happened in there?"

She shrugged, her brow creasing adorably as she gazed up at him with miserable eyes. "I think my father just fell off his pedestal."

He could have told her that happened long ago, but he held his tongue. She adored her dad as much as he loved his mom. Finding out your parents aren't perfect can be a big blow to your world. He'd learned that the hard way when his father was arrested for armed robbery back when he was a kid. One minute they'd been playing baseball in the backyard, and the next the place had swarmed with black and blues. Hurt and confused, he'd refused to go to the prison on visiting days. And then it was too late. His dad died without ever tasting freedom again, and Jason had to live with the black pit of his guilt. Much as he disliked his stepfather, he didn't want Tammy-Jo to go through what he had. He'd learned his lesson. There were no guarantees in life, and it was damn hard to say sorry after a loved one was gone.

"He's probably worried about you. Give him a chance. I imagine he has his hands full now that Hawthorne is dead."

She flinched and he wished the insensitive words back. No one could accuse him of being tactful. "Shit. I'm sorry, honey."

"What do you mean, Dad has his hands full with Tim gone?" She took a step back, bumping into the wall behind her.

He did some quick mental back-pedaling, wondering what she was getting at. "He was your dad's partner, wasn't he?"

Her eyes narrowed and he realized too late he'd made a mistake. "How do you know that, Jason? I never mentioned what Tim did for work, I was too pissed off at him last night for niceties."

Damn, he hated this subterfuge.

He grabbed her arm and marched them down the hall, away from her father's hearing. She glared and broke free. "Do you *mind*?"

He held his hands up and forced a good-old-boy grin he was far from feeling. "Relax. You looked a little off-kilter so I thought I'd be the gentleman and offer my hand. It's no big deal."

"Answer the question, Jason. How did you know Tim worked for my dad?" She crossed her arms and all but tapped her toe.

He grinned. He could totally see her as a sexy librarian.

She sputtered and he did what he'd been wanting to do all morning.

He kissed her.

Chapter Twenty-One

Plastered against Jason's muscular chest, his lips searching hers, Tammy-Jo went from worried, to pulse-pounding panty-dampening lust all in two point five seconds. He'd always had this effect on her. Impossible to resist. Her secret addiction.

Confused thoughts tumbled back and forth in her head like the agitator on a washing machine. Then, nothing was left except this, her and Jason. Together again.

He tasted of mint and coffee and something uniquely belonging to him. Even if she were to lose all of her other senses she would recognize this man

by taste. His mouth was warm and moist. It nourished
her soul like a desert absorbing rain after a long
drought. Her skin blossomed beneath the onslaught,
heating from the inside out. Moaning, she tipped her
face up, her fingers splaying across the expanse of
shoulder to hold her balance in a suddenly topsy-
turvy world.

"I've missed you," he whispered, feathering kisses
along her jaw and the slope of her neck where it met
her shoulder. "We're good together, you and I."

Hands, big and strong, cupped her breasts, calluses
catching on the silky material. He rubbed a nipple and
it swelled, as though seeking his palm. He groaned
and stepped closer, his leg nudging hers apart. She
gasped, as the length of his erection made itself
known along her abdomen. Helpless, she tilted her
pelvis, a desperate hunger to have him inside taking
over her body.

"Jason, please," she panted, lost in a sensual realm
where only the two of them existed. It hurt, this ache
to become one with another human. To offer
everything, body and soul, so that for a few precious

moments you might be lucky enough to leave gravity behind and soar among the clouds. Weightless. To trust in another person enough to take the journey together.

His hand found its way under her dress, fingers sliding along sensitive skin to tease the elastic at the leg of her panties. She twisted and turned, the anxiety building to volcanic proportions.

"Shh, I've got you," he murmured, his voice velvet over gravel.

And he did. The small hairs on the back of his hand rubbed the sensitive skin of her inner thigh, ratcheting the tension. "So perfect. I want to mess you up, T.J. Make you forget everything except me."

Mission accomplished. She couldn't remember her own name right now. She shivered, overtaken by second thoughts. "We should sto... ah," she said as he flicked her clit through the material. He was going to make her come, she could feel it. Right here in the hallway of her father's house.

"Jason." She dropped her hand down to his with the intention of halting this insanity, but she became sidetracked by the feel of his fingers as they moved beneath her panties seeking her core. And then he was delving between the folds. Her muscles constricted, holding him there. She closed her eyes, lost to the exquisite sensations rocking her body.

"Do you like that?" he breathed against her neck.

"Oh God, yes," she moaned.

"Want me to stop?" he asked, his fingers moving away.

She clenched his hand between her thighs. "Don't you dare." She half laughed, half sobbed.

He returned, his thumb unerringly finding her throbbing clit at the same time one, then two fingers slid home. She cried out at the blunt invasion. The wet slide of flesh mixed with the aroma of sex and sweat. She couldn't breathe as he pumped into her, his fingers thick and abrasive. She ground her pelvis against him, her hand moving to wrap as much of the hard length of his cock as she could within the confines of his jeans, mimicking sex with a squeeze and release guaranteed to drive him over the edge.

He jumped and swore under his breath. "You're killing me here." But that didn't stop him from leaning into her touch.

He dropped his dark head to her breast, taking the nipple into his mouth through the silk of her dress and scraping it with his teeth. She bit her lip against the pleasure-pain, afraid she'd scream otherwise, and used her free hand to delve into the thick richness of his hair, holding him in place, not that he seemed in any hurry to leave.

The tension inside her tightened with every shift of their bodies. She was so close, it hurt. "Please," she begged, wanting, needing him with every fiber of her being. She lifted her leg and wrapped it around his hip, dragging him even closer, and gasped as it changed the direction of his fingers, creating little explosions behind her eyes.

"Please what?" he demanded, his voice guttural, thrilling. Eyes indigo blue, flaming hot burned her with their intensity. "Tell me what you want. I need to hear the words, honey."

She could have cried when he withdrew his hand. He was leaving the decision up to her. Was she brave enough to go after what she craved?

"You." She leaned forward, their chests brushing and making both of them shiver in reaction. "I want you, Jason McIntyre." She punctuated the words with kisses everywhere she could reach, his bristly jaw, neck, shoulder, lips. "Every. Single. Solitary. Inch."

Eyes flaring with triumph, his hand gripped the leg she balanced on and lifted. "Hang on, baby. Time to take this party to a more private location."

She squealed and grabbed for his shoulders, her legs scissoring his lean hips. "Hurry," she muttered, anxious to outrun the common sense banging at the door.

***

Jason's heart thundered in his ears. His arms cradled a warm, willing woman. Her intoxicating scent filled his nostrils. It took every ounce of willpower he had left not to push her up against the wall and take her then and there. She deserved more than an illicit fuck in some hallway though. If it were

up to him he'd go the whole nine yards; flowers and
wine, satin sheets and wedding rings.

Yeah, he had it bad.

"Where to?" he asked, assuming she would have a
better idea of a nearby room than he did. The house
had been remodeled since the last time he stayed here.

"Third door on the right," she answered, and did
this shimmy up his torso that set his blood on fire.

He tightened his grip on her ass—not a hardship—
and began the trek to the door she'd pointed out, his
cock swelling painfully in his jeans with the up-down
motion of his footsteps combined with the friction of
her crotch on his.

He wasn't going to make it. He was too close to
the edge.

Sweating he stopped and drew a deep breath,
filling his lungs with the sweet scent of her skin
against his mouth. He nipped her neck and lifted his
head to look deep into her whiskey-colored eyes, now
dark with need.

"Set me down, I'm too heavy." She squirmed and
almost unmanned him right there.

He hissed, his fingers digging into her ass. "Don't move," he warned, "or this party will be over before it begins."

T.J. froze, her gaze turning to confusion, and then the words sank in and she looked down, an amused note entering her voice. "What's the matter, big guy? Can't control yourself?"

He laughed, surprising both of them. "I hope you're talking to me and not Herman down there. He might take offense."

"Well," she said, her eyes sparkling, "if the shoe fits…"

Jason grinned. Damn, he loved this woman. He couldn't remember the last time he laughed while wooing a date. Tammy-Jo was one in a million.

Sobering, he continued down the hall and pushed the door open on a small lounge. One wall was filled floor to ceiling with books while a daybed took up the corner near a big bay window overlooking the trees encompassing the backyard.

He reached back and clicked the lock, the sound loud in the sudden silence. T.J.'s expression changed,

the smile disappearing from lips swollen from his
kisses. A vision of her mouth wrapped around his
cock drew a growl from deep within his chest, and
she jumped, almost loosening herself from his arms.

"Shit, I'm sorry. I didn't mean to scare you," he
said, feeling like a pervert.

She nodded uncertainly, her eyes darting to the bed
and away again. "It's okay, I'm just nervous. It's been
awhile, you know?"

Ten years.

But, then something in her expression gave him
pause. "Like how long?" he asked, his finger grazing
her satiny cheek.

Her lids dropped, the lashes brushing his hand.
"Two years," she said, half under her breath.

A fierce sense of joy filled his chest. Obviously,
she and her husband had been having problems, but
she was willing to entrust him… Jason McIntyre…
with her body.

Tenderness replaced urgency as he feathered soft,
gentle kisses along her forehead, nose, cheeks, chin,

everywhere except her mouth. He was saving the best for last.

Shifting her weight in his hands he carried her to the bed and sat on the edge, her legs on either side of his hips. Relieved of their burden, his hands were free to roam her back, ribcage, the plump fullness of her breasts.

Time slowed.

The tension, when it returned, was different. More like the night sky waiting for the stars to appear. First one, then another, and another, until the atmosphere was lit up as though by thousands of candles, dancing and swaying by the light of the moon until dawn breaks across the sky in a glorious crescendo, bringing forth the promise of a new day with endless possibilities.

He shifted, painfully hard again from mating with her tongue while her fingers played his body like a violin. He wondered if her nipples were the same dusky pink as her lips and worked his magic on her bra, suddenly anxious to find out. Once freed, it was easy work to maneuver them out the top of her dress.

They rested there like a banquet on a shelf, set up for his indulgence.

Ahh, so sweet. Just as pretty as he remembered. Wonder if they were as sensitive as they used to be? He leaned in and blew lightly on one puckered nipple and then the other, smiling faintly when she sucked in a sharp breath which only served to bring the creamy globes closer. Just where he wanted them.

He cradled her breasts in his hands, luxuriating in the soft warmth and the way random shivers chased themselves like mischievous boys across her skin. He wanted to join them, and so he did. Sucking a nipple into his mouth he alternated between nips and licks to heal the little bites and breathing against the nub so that the coolness of the air mixed with the warmth of his mouth in a pleasure-pain. She gasped, her head thrown back, hands clenching and unclenching in his hair as she rode out the exquisite sensations.

She was beautiful.

While he'd been occupied by her pretty titties she'd managed to undo his shirt and the fly of his pants. His cock rose thick and hard between them, the head florid, a tiny pearl of cum resting on the tip. His balls were swollen and aching, nestled in a bed of dark, curly hair.

When he looked up, it was to see her staring, her mouth opened in a delectable ooh, and her eyes wide.

"Don't worry, darlin', it'll fit."

She gave him a saucy smile that almost drove him over the edge. "Ooh, I remember," she said, giving him a little shove that threw him off-balance. He landed with a soft oomph, that made her laugh. "What's the matter big guy, scared of little ol' me?"

As she bent over and took his cock into her mouth, and his eyes rolled back in his head, all he could think was *hell, yeah. Petrified.*

She rolled her tongue under the tip and then down the length and back again before she latched on and sucked, her delicate fingers working him from below and now it was his turn to have quivers jumping under his skin, explosions of ecstasy he couldn't control. Lights strobed behind his eyes, his breath sawing in and out like a freight train. The slide of her teeth down his cock and the warm wetness of her mouth tugging his emotions out through the head, damn near enough to make him pass out.

"T.J.," he moaned, hips flexing. Helpless against the power this one woman welded. His hands fisted in her hair to hold her there, or pull her away, he couldn't say. And then it was too late. His body bowed with the force of the climax, his muscles convulsing as though hit by an electric prod. When it was over, that's how he felt too, weak as a newborn baby, his skin glistening with sweat.

Tammy-Jo climbed up his body and flopped beside him, one leg splayed over his hips, her arm holding him close. Like he mattered to her.

Or so he'd like to believe.

"That was…" she whispered.

"Amazing," he finished, pressing a kiss to her forehead and gratified to taste salty sweetness on his tongue. At least he wasn't the only one.

But, he was getting hard again. Unbelievable.

The feel of her plastered to his side and the musky scent of their combined bodies acted as well as any aphrodisiac sold on the market.

She was his love drug.

It took barely any maneuvering at all to turn his hips enough for his throbbing dick to find her like a magnet finding true north. He slid home with the slightest pressure. God, she was so tight. Sweet perfection.

He rocked his hips, grinding her mons against his cock with ever increasing force. Short, sharp pants penetrated the sensual fog turning him deaf and blind to everything except the coming release. She was close. So close.

He used his arm to lift her leg higher up his ribcage, opening her body further so he could reach her from below, adding his finger to the in, out, drag of his cock. Wet heat. She was so beautifully responsive. Their rhythm a perfect match. Then she did this little twist thing that dragged his thumb across her clit and her channel tightened into a vise, squeezing them into the release they both craved. His eyes closed and he shuddered, entrusting his soul to her body.

They drifted into a boneless sleep.

Later, he lay on his side watching over her as she slept, his heart full. She'd filled out some since they were teenagers stealing kisses where they could. He liked the changes, but mourned the fact he hadn't been here to see them occur. He'd had the dream they would marry, raise happy, healthy kids, and grow old together.

Maybe it wasn't too late. Maybe after this case…

He shut down the forbidden fantasy. When she learned what he'd done, she'd never speak to him again.

Chapter Twenty-Two

Tammy-Jo woke to the afternoon sun streaming through the window above the bed. She opened her eyes and stretched, enjoying the heat on her bare skin. The events of the morning erupted like lightning strikes through her brain. Vignettes of following her father to his office. The drinking and his tense expression when asking for the papers she'd taken. Recognizing their importance to him, though she hadn't known why. Then Jason, tall and dark, appearing out of nowhere. Kissing her. Carrying her away like some damsel in distress. Ravishing her.

Owning her.

Turning her head, she saw what she'd already sensed, he was gone. She lay a few more minutes, basking in the afterglow of the most amazing sex of her life, then rose, wincing at the tenderness between her legs. He hadn't gone easy on her, and she was fiercely glad. She'd caused him to lose control. Her.

No matter what happened between them, she could hold those memories close. He'd laid her dress out across an armchair to avoid wrinkles and placed her shoes neatly below. The simple act brought tears to her eyes. He was such a contradiction. Arrogant and cocky one minute, diffident and kind the next. Life with Jason McIntyre would never be boring. And she wished with all her heart this time he'd give her the chance to find out if she was right.

Buoyed by the possibilities, she hurried into her clothes and hand-brushed her hair, hoping she wasn't too late to join him and Caroline for dinner. She stopped to straighten the pillows on the daybed, holding one to her nose and catching the faint scent of Jason's spicy pine cologne. It *had* really happened. Her body told her so, but she'd been half afraid to believe it. She hugged the pillow, then reluctantly let it go. She needed to get moving if she wanted time for a shower.

Thank goodness, the hall was empty when she opened the door. No fancy explanations necessary. Still, she forced her strides to be sedate and calm until she reached the stairs. Then, she pulled off her shoes, held them by their glossy red heels, and raced up the curved wooden treads as though she were a schoolkid.

By the time she arrived at her room and closed the door, she was breathless and giggling like a lunatic. It had been a long time since she felt this light-hearted. Since Jason.

Sobering, T.J. dropped her shoes on the silly white Persian carpet and walked through to the washroom, the fur bunching beneath her toes. Maybe she was making too much from their union. Why hadn't he woken her up before he left? It would have saved her from all these wishy-washy feelings squirming inside her chest. Dammit, she wasn't fifteen anymore. If she wanted an affair with a handsome journalist here for a

short time, not a long time, then she'd darn well have
one.

She twisted the two-carat diamond on her ring
finger. It wasn't as though she was married anymore.
Yanking the gaudy wedding band off, she set it on the
counter and shed her walk-of-shame clothes before
climbing into the shower. The warm water soothed
sore muscles. Faint smudges appeared on her breasts
and arms and inner thighs. He'd left his mark on her.
She stilled, suddenly realizing they hadn't used
protection. She was clean, obviously. Tim hadn't
touched her in years, she hadn't let him. But, what
about Jason? She had no idea what his usual modus
operandi was like.

How careless.

What if she was pregnant? A sharp thrill
whispered up her spine and her hand went
protectively to her flat stomach. Not likely. Not after
just one night, but it was possible. Birth control pills
made her sick so she'd stopped taking them after the
breakdown of her marriage. There'd been no need.
Until now.

She dropped her hand and hurried through the rest
of her ablutions. *"Don't be silly,"* she told herself.
*"You can't tell something that important just because
you feel... different."* No, she couldn't, but it didn't
hurt to dream.

Drying off, she returned to the bedroom in search
of something to wear, grateful to see her father's maid
had cleaned her dress from last night's tragedy. She'd
have to find out how long before the police would let
her back into her house. She couldn't keep wearing
the same clothes, and unless she wanted to ask her
father for a loan, she was essentially broke. Hard to
imagine, her entire world had been flipped on its side
in under twenty-four hours. No wonder she was a hot
mess.

About to leave the room, T.J. glanced over her
shoulder to the neatly made bed. She should take the
documents to her father, but something made her
hesitate. She didn't like how desperate he'd seemed.
There was more to those numbers than she was
seeing. Maybe later, when they came back after

dinner, she could bring Jason to her room and get his opinion.

Yeah, right. Who was she fooling? Now she was making excuses to see him again.

You are pathetic.

No, she was in love. And this time, she had no intention of letting him disappear from her life.

The house was quiet as she descended the stairs and hurried to the kitchen. She'd taken too long, they'd left without her. Deflated, she turned to go back to her room when she noticed a note propped against a cup on the table.

Decided to let you sleep.

A warm glow suffused her chest.

If you see this, we're at the Kingsman. Meet us there.

Jason

A set of keys lay beside the note. Mustang car keys. He'd left her his car. It was impossible to suppress the hope that bloomed. He loved his car. He wouldn't lend it to just anyone, right? It felt like a declaration.

God, she hoped so.

Eager to see him and find out for sure, she
snatched up the keys, her grip so tight they bit into
her palm, and tip-toed through the house to the front
door. The last thing she wanted was to run into her
father right now. He'd never understand her urgency
to see Jason and she didn't need a lecture.

She breathed a sigh of relief once the door closed
behind her. The car sat in the driveway where they'd
left it the night before. T.J. hoped she remembered the
lessons Jason had given her years ago on how to drive
a standard or this was going to be a short trip.

She opened the door with the remote and was
about to climb in when a masculine hand caught her
arm, stopping the motion. Startled she gave a yelp,
and turned to look into a face only a mother could
love. A hooked nose sat between narrow, squinty
brown eyes. The man's cheeks were pock-marked, his
skin ruddy. He looked to be mid-forties and no one
she'd ever seen before. She'd have remembered.

"Sorry, miss," he said, trying on a smile that came nowhere near his eyes. "Can I speak with yous a minute?"

Nervous, she glanced around for help, but the street was empty. "Who are you? What do you want?" She forcibly removed her arm, wincing when the skin twisted under his grip before he let her go.

He stepped back a pace, but was still too close for comfort.

"Let's just say we have a mutual friend." He wiped that honker of a nose with a soiled handkerchief. Her stomach rebelled. "You have something he wants and he's willing to pay for it." He leaned into her face, his breath stinking of peppermint and tobacco. "I recommend you take his offer." He slid a card down the front of her dress, smirked and walked away whistling.

Tammy-Jo stared until long after he disappeared around the corner, her heart fluttering wildly in her breast. Finally, she calmed enough to pull the card from her neckline, shuddering at the remembered touch of his fingers against her skin.

She held the card up, half expecting it to burst into flames, but all that it held was a phone number and the brief message; *Don't make me wait.*

Oh my god. What had she gotten herself into?

Chapter Twenty-Three

"Can you see what she's holding?" Cam asked from over Dani's shoulder. His closeness bothered her. Everything about the man bothered her. And made her hot.

Irritated, she shifted in the driver's seat of the van, knocking the focus out on the binoculars. Pissed, she turned her head to glare up at her boss. "If I knew, I'd tell you. Now back off and give me some room, unless you want these?" She lifted the glasses from their perch on top the steering wheel and shoved them towards him.

Cam lifted his hands, one clutching the ever-present cell phone, and took a step back, clunking his head on the roof. He cursed under his breath and rubbed his scalp. "Relax, Martel. It was a simple question."

Dani huffed, exasperated. Why did she always leap onto the defensive around him? Her attitude made things awkward for the entire team. It would be her own fault if she was transferred.

"Sorry," she muttered, and avoided his questioning gaze by turning back to their quarry across the street, goggles firmly in place. "I think it's a card. She's looking at it now. Man, that guy threw her for a loop. She's whiter than my t-shirt." She glanced at Cam, the smirk dying when she saw where his attention had gone.

Her chest.

She looked down to see if she'd spilled coffee again or something, but no, for once there were no stains on the V-neck cotton she preferred for these surveillance trips. It got damn hot in this coffin on four wheels, especially if they had to put in many

hours, and she didn't plan on stinking the place up.
Leave that to the men.

"I'm worried about Steve," she said, lowering the
glasses once more to cross her arms over her chest.
Just because they'd had a short, intense fling, it didn't
give Cam the right to ogle her, dammit.

He frowned, whether at her words or her actions,
she wasn't sure. "He'll be fine. He's a big boy, even
if he doesn't act it half the time."

He came forward invading her space as he
squeezed past to climb into the passenger seat. His
jean-clad thigh brushed her arm before she could
draw away, causing a frisson of awareness she was
helpless to ignore. While her knees dropped neatly
over the edge of her seat, his were barely an inch
from the glovebox. His shoulders curved inward as he
checked the GPS on his phone, but even then, they
took up more than their share of the space.

He angled the phone in her direction. "See, he's
still on the move." He met her gaze, his eyes a warm
sherry brown with a dark ring around the iris.
Mesmerizing.

Dani cleared her throat and slumped back in her chair. "How do you know that proves anything? He could be stuffed in that creep's trunk and getting driven to the swamp even as we speak."

Cam's lips quirked. "The swamp? You been reading those murder mysteries again, Martel?"

She couldn't help it, she blushed. He'd remembered her penchant for whodunits. "You should try one sometime. You could learn all sorts of stuff." The words hardly left her lips when she realized just how they sounded. Her blush turned fire engine red.

He looked at her fiery face and a smile cracked those austere cheeks.

Mesmerizing? How about spellbinding.

The man could grace a GQ cover if he did that more often. She was kind of glad he didn't. Or at least not that she'd seen. Which led her to wondering about his private life. They'd never gotten around to talking…

"He sent a mayday ping. Let's go."

The words were a splash of cold water on her heated thoughts. Dani darted a worried glance at Cam's phone, then started the van with a muted roar and pulled out onto the road, driving past the Hawthorne woman still standing in the driveway beside Jason's car. Had he given it to her to drive? If he had, things were much more serious between them than he'd let on. Dani didn't know how she was supposed to feel about that. Right now, she was totally freaking out about Steve.

"Take the next right. Easy," Cam growled as she took the corner too fast and the van leaned dangerously into the curve.

"You do your thing, and I'll do mine," she snapped back, her adrenaline through the roof. Jason had spent hours teaching her and Steve offensive driving. She remembered laughing and asking him, "Isn't that *defensive driving?*"

He'd replied, "Defensive is for safety. I want you to learn how to rule the road." And he hadn't let up on them until he was satisfied. "You never know

when it might come in handy, especially with our
job."

She was pretty freaking grateful to him right now.
The van zipped in and out of the sporadic traffic on
the street like an Indy sports car. The traffic light
ahead was green, but she had more than half a block
to go before she was through and there was no way
she was going to sit at a red, so she dropped a gear
and punched the gas. The powerful engine leaped the
vehicle forward like a giant cat pouncing on its prey.

"You trying to get us killed?" Cam said, arms
braced, one on the door, and the other on the dash.

She grinned as they blew through the yellow,
horns clashing behind them. She'd made him
nervous. The big boss-man wasn't as tough as he
portrayed. For some reason that made her happy.

"You're still here, aren't ya?" she said, giving
herself a mental high five. Then she heard another
ping come in on his cellphone and the humor died.

"How far away are we?" she asked, scared to hear
the answer.

He met her worried glance, his face stern. But now she knew it was worry for his team that made him look that way.

"Too damn far. Punch it."

Chapter Twenty-Four

Jason guided his mother into a booth at the
Kingsman pub and hotel. He had an ulterior motive in
bringing her here today. He'd hoped that seeing the
restaurant where she'd worked for much of his
formative years would trigger happy memories. But,
though she was polite to the server and commented
on the polished mahogany bar that ran the length of
the back wall separating customers from liquor
bottles of every shape and description, there was no
sign she remembered the long shifts, or sore feet
she'd regularly come home with after a busy
nightshift.

"This is nice," she said, her fingers fiddling with the cutlery wrapped in a burgundy linen napkin. Her gaze was nervous as she surveyed the other diners. "Do you come here often?"

Well, not in the last ten years. "Once in a while." He kept his answer noncommittal. "They cook a good steak." He grinned when she turned up her dainty nose. She'd never been much of a red meat eater. "Salads too."

She looked at him and smiled. His heart flopped clean over.

"You're teasing me now." She laughed, setting the cutlery aside to look at the menu. "Just because I don't like my meat to moo at me," she said, referring to his preference for rare steaks, "doesn't mean I don't eat beef. I think I'll have the meat loaf." She looked up and met his befuddled gaze. Her lips straightened. "What? Is there something wrong with my choice?"

He shook his head. "No, that sounds perfect to me." How could she remember the way he liked his steak, but not the place she'd worked? There was no rhyme nor reason to dementia. It was a war he couldn't win and it frightened him.

The server returned to take their orders, leaving an awkward silence after he left. Jason didn't know where to steer the conversation for fear of upsetting her. So, he waited, hoping she'd take the lead.

"Is your girlfriend joining us?" she finally asked, looking as uncomfortable as he felt. Maybe this wasn't such a good idea.

"I'm not sure. She was taking a nap when we left." And if his mother hadn't been waiting, he'd have been there to wake her up.

Tammy-Jo surprised him. He hadn't expected her to explode in his arms the way she had. There'd been no going back after that. It was a damn good thing there'd been a room nearby before he'd totally lost control. They hadn't even used a condom. He couldn't believe it. He hadn't done anything that irresponsible since he was a teenager. What was she going to think of him now?

"Oh, look, there are the Donaldsons." His mother interrupted his thoughts, her face shining like a

welcoming beacon. She lifted her hand to get the
attention of an older couple who changed direction to
wind through the tables to their booth.

"Caroline, so good to see you," the woman said,
leaning down to brush a kiss along her cheek. The
scent of Chanel drifted across the table. Not that
Jason needed that to tell him they were moneyed. The
jewels on every finger and diamonds in her ears
practically shouted money while her linen dress and
fashionable pumps said understated elegance. He was
instantly curious about their connection to his mother.

She turned, and he was startled by her shark-eyed
gaze. Eyes, a cold, flat gray inspected him from head
to toe and then dismissed him. A shiver raised the
hairs on the back of his neck. Who *were* these
people?

"And who is this handsome man you have with
you? Have you been holding out on us, dear? Does
Sam know you're out with a stranger?" Her voice
reminded him of a snake. She stretched out the s's as
though savoring the taste of each word. He didn't like
her.

"Don't be rude, Martha. Give Caroline a chance to answer." Her companion offered his hand. "Sebastian Donaldson. This ill-mannered woman is my wife, Martha."

Jason shook the other man's hand, surprised by his firm grip. Something about these two raised all his warning flags. Time to do a little digging.

He stood and offered the battle-axe… Martha, his chair. "Please, join us."

Triumph glittered in the steel traps of her eyes. "Thank you. We will." She took a seat and lifted her hand imperiously for the server. "Two more chairs, and hurry it up would you. We don't have all day."

The man who'd been polite and smiling while taking their order earlier now wore a face carved from granite. "Yes, *ma'am,*" he stressed. "Right away." He gave Jason a glance rife with sarcasm and pulled a one-eighty so sharp his heels clicked together. Jason's military buddies would've been impressed.

Aware they were quickly becoming the main attraction at this circus, he smiled to ease the worry furling his mother's brow. "So, Mom, tell me where

you met this couple." He caught the glance Martha
and her husband shared. Good. These two needed to
know his mother wasn't some easy pawn in whatever
game they were playing. The more he saw, the more
he was convinced they hadn't befriended her out of
compassion. They were up to something.

The server returned with the extra chairs and set
the table to accommodate their guests. He took the
drink orders and Jason was amused to hear Martha
demanding a dirty martini—how appropriate.

When they were alone again, Martha leaned across
the table and patted his mother's hand. "Let me tell
the story, Caroline. I know you get confused." The
words were said kindly, but that didn't stop the
stricken look on Caroline's face. Jason wanted to rip
the woman's head off and shit down the hole. Where
did she get off upsetting his mom that way?

"Mom…"

Her smile was a timid facsimile of the ones they'd
shared earlier. "It's all right. Let M… Martha explain.
She'll be much better at it than I will."

Jason's jaw ached from gritting his teeth. He glanced at the viper's husband, but the man was smiling and sipping on his scotch as though nothing was wrong. Either that or he was well used to his wife's domineering ways.

"Sebastian and I are old acquaintances of Samuel's."

Why didn't that surprise him?

She took a dainty sip of her cocktail, pinky finger crooked like she was waiting for her pet bat to land. When she set the drink down, the pink outline of her lip remained on the glass. Orchestra music piped in through speakers set discreetly into the ceiling added to the whole kitschy vibe he was getting from these two. It was like they'd stepped out of a *film noir*; he was waiting for her to pull a derringer out of her purse.

"Sebastian is a business associate of your… step-father, is it?" She tipped her head to the side as though curious, but Jason had a feeling she already knew the answer. The question was, what else did she know?

He nodded and gave his mom a reassuring smile. "That's right. Mom and Sam got married when I was a teenager. They've been together ever since."

Martha turned to Caroline. "Oh yes, it was a Cinderella story, wasn't it? Samuel met and fell for the pretty waitress and whisked her and her troubled child off to a life of luxury. They could make a Hallmark movie out of your tale." She clapped her hands in glee.

Jason glowered at the customers staring at their table. "Do you have a point to this?" he asked, tempted to hustle his mom out the door.

Just then their meals arrived. The steak he'd been looking forward to now made his stomach roil. He could see the same reaction from his mother, but the Donaldsons tucked into their lamb chops with gusto.

Was it too much to hope they choked?

Sebastian glanced up, a forkful of food hovering in the air between them. "What's the matter, old son? Steak not to your liking?"

No, the company wasn't to his liking.

"It's fine," he said. "Where did you say you met
Sam?" Maybe they were investors in his step-father's
Ponzi scheme and could help their case.

Surprisingly, it was Caroline who spoke. "I
introduced them." She looked at Martha fondly. "A
couple of years ago, Sam and I took a cruise to
Alaska." She turned to meet his gaze, her eyes soft
with memories. "You know how he is, work, work,
work." She smiled. "I got fed up one night and took a
walk on our deck. Silly me, I ended up lost. Martha
and her husband took pity and helped me find my
way back to our suite. I invited them in for a drink,
and, as they say, the rest is history."

And, a little too convenient.

He turned to Sebastian. "I missed what kind of
business you're involved with?"

The other man set his fork down to wipe his lips
on the linen napkin before answering. "Stocks, bonds,
a little of this and that. I'm what you might call an
financier. You do know what that is, I assume?" He
raised his brow and took another drink of the nearly
empty scotch.

"Sure," Jason said. "You're a mercenary."

Martha gasped.

Sebastian sputtered, his drink spraying from his mouth in a fine mist that covered his food.

Caroline's eyes rounded in surprise, but then she shook her head and her lips quirked in an amused smile.

Jason winked and took a swig of his beer.

Take that, *old man.*

Chapter Twenty-Five

Tammy-Jo wandered back into her father's house in a daze. The stranger had destroyed the euphoric feeling she'd woken up with and left fear and uncertainty in its place. What should she do? That warning, *Don't make me wait…* She shuddered, picturing Tim as she'd seen him last, zipped into a black body bag.

The house was cool and shaded, the blinds pulled against the afternoon sunlight. She wanted to run to every window and open them wide, banishing the darkness, but then she thought of who could be watching and was thankful for the privacy.

She locked the door and set the alarms, something her family never did during the day, and returned to the kitchen. Set at the back of the house, it seemed to offer the greatest security from would-be intruders. It had always been her favorite room, the place where busy people became a family. She could barely recall her mother, but the memories she had were tied up in this room. The warm, yeasty scent of bread rising on the counter, a towel covering the doughy ball like a baby put down for a nap. The love and the laughter— always the laughter. Her father would often sweep her mom into his arms, floury hands and all, and dance around the room humming a tune that made her smile. Then it was T.J.'s turn. He'd hold her hands and get her to stand on his feet and away they'd go, the sun glinting through the big bay window over the sink turning the room into prisms of light like something out of a fairytale.

But then her mom got sick and the laughter was gone.

T.J. shook her head. It had been a long time since she'd remembered those days. They'd been happy then, the three of them. She was just glad her dad had found someone new to love, and Caroline was great. She'd been kindness itself from the first day they met. It couldn't have been easy getting saddled by a hormonal teen with a gigantic chip on her shoulder. She cringed, thinking about some of the things she'd said and done back then. The woman deserved a medal for sticking around.

She turned on the tap and stared out the back window. All the lots on this street backed onto the Kanawha State Forest Park so they had complete privacy—something she appreciated now. Wood Warblers flitted among the branches of the trees and the meadow leading up to the fence line was filled with wildflowers of every color and description. They'd camped in the park a few times, though her father had been too busy to take them most summers. After her mother died, he'd sold the camping trailer and they'd never gone back.

The cool water slid down her throat and helped bolster her courage enough to take another look at the card that man had forced onto her. It was made of heavyweight stock and advertised the Magnolia Country Club, of all things. Was it a coincidence, or could the club somehow be tied up in this mess?

Or was there a more sinister message attached to the note? One that suggested whoever this was knew her routines, maybe had even been there yesterday when she'd been asked to leave? She flipped the card over and read the frightening words again. Her mind skipped to the next most obvious conclusion; was this the person behind Tim's death?

"I thought you were bringing me those papers." A man's voice, heavy with annoyance, sounded from behind her.

T.J. screamed and dropped her water glass, shattering it on the kitchen tiles. Shards of glass bit the skin of her legs, the blood mixing with the rivulets of water dripping into her shoes.

She started to turn and her father yelled, "Hold still, for god's sake, before you make it worse."

Violent shivers wracked her body, but she obeyed her dad's command and froze, watching as he awkwardly swept the mess away with a broom.

"Sorry, Daddy, I don't know why I jumped that way." She was embarrassed now that she knew Tim's killer wasn't in the room. Talk about an active imagination.

Her father grunted. "Sit down and let's have a look at your legs. We need to get the glass out." He nodded toward a chair and crunched his way over to the sink to wash his hands.

Feeling like a troublesome child, T.J. sat on the edge of the chair and grimaced at the soggy mess her shoes were in.

"I'm fine," she said, plucking a small sliver from her calf. Blood trickled from the wound, turning her stomach. She never could stand seeing anyone cut.

Her dad kneeled at her side and brushed her hand away. He used a dry tea towel to catch the flow, then removed a couple more shards and repeated the motion. When he was satisfied, he handed her the towel and clambered to his feet.

"You about scared me plumb to death, daughter," he said, wiping his brow. She remembered he wasn't

a fan of blood either. Guess that's where she got it
from.

"Bad nerves, I guess. I was thinking about what
happened to Tim and then your voice came out of
nowhere and gave me a heart attack." She laughed.

He nodded, his gaze sympathetic as it rested on her
face. "Don't worry, punkin. The *po*-lice will catch
whoever it was and life will go back to normal."

Normal.

What was her normal going to be now that her
husband was dead and her assets frozen? It was
unlikely the lawyers would look favorably upon the
dislodged wife of a former hustler. Now he was gone
she could acknowledge it to herself. There'd been
signs, harsh phone calls late at night, quick trips
abroad, money they shouldn't have had. But she'd
turned a blind eye, unwilling to stir the pot on their
already uncertain marriage. Then, he'd gone ahead
and ripped the lid right off that sucker. In front of
three hundred of their closest acquaintances, no less.

Good thing he was dead. She'd been tempted to
murder him herself.

"What is this?"

Her dad's voice recalled her to the room. She looked over and sucked in a swift breath. He was holding the card from the county club in his hand, a deep frown furrowing his brow.

"Is someone threatening you?" he asked, waving the wet card in the air like a town crier.

Damn, she must have dropped it in her fright. She thought fast. "It's a catering company, Dad. I was looking into a dinner party for you and Caroline's anniversary next month. This guy is busy so he needs an answer soon, that's all."

His shoulders relaxed. "Caroline will love that, you know how she is with parties." He smiled and handed her the card, then continued cleaning up the broken glass from the floor.

"If this fellow gives you a tough time, tell him to come to me. You have enough on your plate right now."

Wasn't that the truth?

Chapter Twenty-Six

The mood inside the SEC van was tense as Dani drove through the busy streets of Magnolia searching for a needle in a freaking haystack. They had no idea what they were looking for; car, truck, van. It frustrated the hell out of her not having a clear target. Steve's life depended on her and Cam making the right decisions. No pressure.

"Where are they?" she growled, her fingers white on the steering wheel.

"We'll find them," Cam answered, his gaze on the little red dot blinking across the map on his phone. "We're closing in on them now."

Not fast enough.

They didn't even know if Steve was still alive. These people were desperate. They'd made that abundantly clear when they decided to off one of the key investors in the group.

"Stop," Cam roared. His gaze was frantic as he scanned the side street they'd just passed. "Back up. Hurry. He's down that alley."

Oh, God, oh, God. Her heart was ready to jump out of her chest and fly ahead of them. *Please, let Steve be okay. Please.*

She kept the silent mantra up as she nailed the brakes and threw the van into reverse before shoving the gas pedal through the floorboard. The momentum propelled her body over top of the steering wheel, her butt taking air, then back with a slam, her head bearing the brunt as it connected with the headrest. But Jason would be proud. She kept control of the wheel and all four tires going where she asked them to.

The alley came up fast. She cranked the wheel hard to the right, and they were in, leaving a stripe of

white paint along the brick wall of a Chinese
restaurant. The alley was long and narrow. Driving it
was made tougher by cars and scooters parallel
parked alongside, interspersed by the odd waste bin
angled so that the edge stuck out like a can opener.
There were lights ahead, but she couldn't tell if it was
one vehicle or more. She rolled down her window,
then wished she hadn't as the mixed stench of stir fry,
oil, and garbage wafted into the cab.

"You're doing great, honey. We'll get him, just
hang in there a few more minutes, okay?" Cam
squeezed her arm in reassurance. His eyes were a
quick flash of warmth in the darkness before he
focused out the windshield again, as though he could
mentally tow the other vehicle to a standstill.

And maybe it worked.

Brake lights lit up the walls and flashed off chrome
bumpers. They cast an eerie red glow on the
horrifying scene unfolding before their eyes.

The back door of the dark sedan—maybe a
Chevy?—swung open and a body tipped out like a
drunk falling off his chair. It hit the ground, bounced,

then lay there unmoving. The car picked up speed and swayed around a corner at the end of the street, the door banging shut like a gunshot.

Dani didn't wait for direction, she slammed on the brakes and was out of the van before it quit moving.

"Martel, wait," Cam called, his voice harsh behind her. He grabbed her arm, causing her to stumble and almost go down. "Dani, I said wait." He saved her from falling only to thrust her against the nearby wall, her cheek scraping the rough brick.

Furious, she jerked free and gave his annoyingly muscular chest a shove, to which he answered by moving not an inch. *Err.*

"Get out of my way, Donovan," she snapped. "Don't you even care that Steve's lying there *hurt*?"

Cam looked down at her and the disappointment in his gaze tightened her throat.

"Steve's my friend too, Danielle, but it's *my* job to make sure my crew is safe." He glanced at the fallen man before turning back to her. "I've already let one teammate down, I'm not letting anyone else get injured. Not on my watch."

His eyes scanned the area again, his body poised to explode into whatever action he deemed necessary. Guilt flooded her chest. Of course he cared about Steve, they'd been friends long before *she* came along. She was the interloper, the one working to fit in, to be an active and valuable member to the team. If she didn't tear them all apart first.

"What do you want me to do?" she asked. Not exactly an apology, but the best she could muster at the moment.

He nodded, accepting the unspoken attempt at conciliation. "Stay here." She sputtered and he raised his hand for silence. "Give me time to scout the area. We need to make sure our suspect hasn't circled back, ready to pick us off like shooting ducks in a barrel." He cupped her chin. "Please, honey. I couldn't handle it if you got hurt."

He dropped a swift kiss on her lips and then he was gone, becoming one with the lengthening afternoon shadows turning the normal city backstreet alley into something otherworldly and mysterious.

Alone, every little sound seemed amplified, from the cawing of a crow overhead to the muted noise of the traffic flowing by the yawning mouth of the road. A door banged and she just about jumped out of her skin, barely restraining the yelp that would have put paid to her cover and possibly endanger Cam's life. A man wearing a soiled butcher's apron stepped outside carrying what looked to be a weighty bag of garbage. He glared at their van sitting on the street between him and the waste bin before hefting the bag higher and stomping around back of the vehicle. He reappeared a moment later at the bin, then heaved the bag up and over the top where it landed with a soft thump. He shook his head at the van again, then stomped around front this time, briefly cutting across the headlights—Dani remembered she'd left it running—then stalked back into his store, apparently without noticing the man lying unconscious on the street a mere half block away.

She touched trembling fingers to her lips. Much as she ached to rush to Steve's side, she'd wait. And watch. And pray like she'd never prayed before.

Chapter Twenty-Seven

Jason drove home in silence. He was afraid if he started grilling his mother about the Donaldsons, he'd upset her. He'd snapped a couple of pictures with his cell phone and forwarded them to Dani for evaluation. She was one of the best in the biz at facial recognition. Her program analyzing characteristics, unique demographics, and emotional triggers was used widely in the security industry. If anyone could figure out who those two were, it was Dani.

He turned the radio on to a jazz station and glanced at his mom, but she was in a world of her own, a slight smile turning her face soft and dreamy.

He much preferred that look to when she felt lost and confused. He wished he had the power to slay her dragons in those moments. The specialists had warned them each case was different. Some patients enjoyed fairly normal lives for years, while others slipped away almost in front of their loved one's eyes. There were studies linking dementia to diabetes and an insensitivity to insulin but there was no cure for either condition. At least the disease seemed to be moving slowly—for now.

Tammy-Jo hadn't shown up at the restaurant. Maybe she'd missed his note or was still sleeping. He stepped a little harder on the gas pedal, the thought of being the one to wake her tempting him past the posted speed limit. They could pick up where they'd left off, in his room this time. The hotel he'd booked featured a spa bath in each room. He could think of all sorts of ways to enjoy his stay in Magnolia.

If only he wasn't investigating her father.

Maybe it wasn't too late, he could get himself removed from the case and take his mom and T.J. on a vacation. He had holidays coming and Sam couldn't begrudge him some time with his family. It was the perfect solution.

Except, if there was one thing he'd learned, running wasn't the answer.

Somehow, some way, he was going to have to come clean and confess his real reason for returning home; if only it didn't feel like the harbinger of doom. His mother might forgive him, though his confession would hurt her, but he was scared he'd lose Tammy-Jo forever.

Horns blared and he jerked, reflexively slamming on the brakes and throwing an arm out to stop his mom's forward momentum. What the...?

She gasped and gaped at him, her hand fluttering to her chest. "What happened? Is there an accident?"

Jason did a quick head-to-toe check verifying she hadn't been injured, then shook his head, his gaze searching cars for the cause of the pileup. "I'm not sure. I don't see..."

Suddenly, out of his peripheral vision he saw a sight that made his pulse jump. The news van the SEC was using for cover sped down the street dodging cars like it was the Indianapolis 500. They must have run a red light, hence the horn-blaring. Something was going down and he needed to be there.

Except he had his mom in the car. He couldn't leave her on the street, not in her condition. Dammit. He had no choice.

"Mom," he said, already inching his way through the maze of angry motorists. "My friends are in trouble. I have to help them."

As if she did high speed chases every day of the week, Caroline buckled up and braced herself against the door. "Of course you do. Let's go, son."

She never failed to amaze him. He flashed her a grin meant to reassure, but probably came out more roguish excitement.

"Hang on, this might get rough." She nodded and he focused his attention on following the quickly disappearing van in front of them. He hoped no pedestrians stepped out as stores and intersections whizzed by at an alarming speed. Cam would never risk public safety this way unless it was necessary.

Maybe they'd caught a break on the killer. He tried
calling Dani via the Bluetooth in his car, but it
skipped over to voicemail. What the hell was
happening?

He glanced at his mom; her face was pale, but
otherwise she seemed to be holding it together
admirably well. No time like the present for
confessing, at least some of the facts.

"Mom, I have something to tell you," he started,
picking up even more speed to beat the light that had
just turned yellow.

"Eyes on the road, son," she warned.

He grinned. "Yes, ma'am." She was impressing
the hell out of him. He'd be happy to have her as his
co-pilot any day of the week. As long as they weren't
chasing down dangerous suspects, that is. He waited
until he'd cleared the light before starting again.

"I'm not a reporter, Mom. That white van up there
is government issue. My teammates and I are part of
an investigative arm of the U.S. Securities and
Exchange Commission. It's our job to close down
white-collar crime." He glanced over to see if she

grasped what he was saying. "Do you know what that is, Mom?"

She rolled her eyes at him. "I wasn't born yesterday. Of course, I know what that is. Now please, pay attention to the road." Her volume rose at the end when he narrowly missed plowing into the back of a Smart car driving like five miles an hour.

Grateful for the responsive steering on his Mustang, he wheeled into the other lane and passed the misnamed vehicle without mishap. Up ahead, the van slammed on its brakes. Reverse lights came on, it backed up a few feet and then wheeled into a side street and disappeared between the buildings. Jason glanced over his shoulder and swore. Thanks to the shitbox he'd swerved to avoid and the congested traffic, he was now in the wrong lane to make that turn. He'd have to continue past and try to catch up on the other end.

"Do you know where that street comes out, Mom?" he asked, searching for a break in the flow.

She looked out the side window as they raced by and nodded. "Take a right at the intersection two blocks from here. These are one-ways, we can catch up to your friends on Seymour Street."

Right, he'd forgotten the town had incorporated one-ways into their infrastructure when the business core became too busy to handle the traffic. "Perfect. You make a great navigator," he told her and caught her smile out the corner of his eye. Warmth flooded his chest. They were bonding. Not exactly the way most families did it, but that's okay. This was the closest they'd been in more years than he could remember. As long as he wasn't placing her in harm's way with this chase.

"Look," he said, spying a space in the gridlock and slipping into the slot. "When we get to where we're going I need you to stay in the car and lock the doors. No matter what, you got that, Momma?"

When she didn't answer he looked over and was dismayed to see the familiar confused, slightly frightened look in her eyes.

"What's going on, Jason?" Her voice had turned quivery, almost childlike.

He forced a smile around the lump in his throat. "Nothing, Ma. We're out for a drive, that's all. Just a drive."

Shit, he should give up the chase and take her home. But what if his team needed him? He couldn't decide what he should do.

The phone rang, startling both of them. He clicked the control on the steering wheel and Dani's panicked whisper filled the car. "Jason, where the hell are you? We have a situation. I need you here like yesterday."

His pulse picked up the pace at her words and he took the corner at the intersection as his mom had suggested, praying he wouldn't live to regret it.

"I'm nearby. I saw you barrel through on Main Street and followed, but lost sight when you took that alley. Give me your ten-twenty and I'll be there as soon as I can." He reached over and grasped his mom's chilled fingers, squeezing gently.

"We're still in the alley. We were watching your prissy girlfriend when some guy approached, gave her something and took off. Steve followed and was grabbed. They dumped him out of a dark car, possibly

a Chev, and now he's lying on the road not moving.
Cam told me to hold position, but I'm so worried.
What if he's bleeding out or something? I don't know
what to do." The words tripped over themselves and
Jason could hear the fear in her voice.

"Do what Cam says. I'm just around the corner.
Hang on, okay?" He dropped a gear and hit the gas,
causing the car to fishtail before straightening out and
shooting down the road like an arrow. Thankfully,
this side street was considerably quieter than the main
drag. Now to intersect with the one-way.

"Hurry, Jason. Please," Dani said before cutting
their connection.

He checked to see if his mom had understood any
of the conversation, but she looked as confused as he
felt. What did T.J. have to do with this case? And
Dodger... Christ. Whoever it was had to have gotten
the drop on him. Steve held a blackbelt in
Taekwondo; he was a formidable opponent. Cam
would be going nuts right now. He took every injury
of a team member as if it were his own. And if Steve
was dead...

Jason didn't even want to contemplate that scenario. They'd been friends for a long time. All of them. Dani was the newest member and she'd been there three years already.

"Jason."

His mom interrupted his thoughts. He glanced her way.

"Isn't that the dark car your friend mentioned a moment ago?" She pointed to an Impala driving erratically down the one-way running in the opposite direction. The one flowing away from the alley.

Holy shit, she was right.

"Mom, you're a natural at this," he hooted and pulled a sharp ninety to fall into line behind their suspect.

"What about the girl?" she asked, white fingers clenching the dash in a death hold.

His job was to capture the criminal. Cam and Dani were on scene to help Steve. He'd leave his friend's care in their capable hands. But, just in case… He handed her his cell phone.

"Call the police, tell them where they are and that there are possible injuries." Satisfied, he'd done the best he could with a bad situation, Jason kept a tail on the car in front of him.

Chapter Twenty-Eight

Leo tugged the ball cap lower and kept a close watch on the speed limit and his rear-view mirror. Attracting the attention of a patrol officer was the last thing he needed right now.

He'd screwed up, no two ways about it.

He should have stuck with the script; given the Hawthorne woman her warning and gotten the hell out of there. And he would have done just that if he hadn't felt that Fed on his ass. He'd been tempted to drop him right there. A bullet between the eyes like he'd done for good ol' Timothy would have been a lot less complicated.

Instead, he'd decided to have a little fun and see what government agency was watching the Hawthorne place. Maybe use the info later as barter, but it hadn't worked out that way.

First of all, the asshole trailing him was a hell of a lot tougher than he looked. If not for the Taser, Leo wasn't sure he could have taken him. And it turned out he wasn't alone. Should have known, the government was filled with pansies needing their hands held.

But now he had a problem.

He needed a place to hole up until the heat died down, and he was short on cash. The payments hadn't appeared as promised. He took another glance in the rear-view and hesitated on a black Mustang that was following about three cars back. There'd been one like it the night of the murder. And he didn't believe in coincidences.

Time to get out of Dodge.

***

After his mom made the call to the police, Jason tried Dani again.

She answered on the first ring. "I hope you're calling to say you're right around the corner, McIntyre, 'cause that's the only thing I want to hear."

That was his Dani, full of attitude. She sounded a lot better than their last phone call. Not so freaked out. He hoped that meant good things for Steve.

"Not quite. I picked up that Chevy you mentioned. We're tailing about three cars back and heading due west. Backup is on the way." He heard the first of the sirens and sighed with relief. "I repeat, backup is on the way. Do Not Move until they get there. You hear me, Martel?"

There were a few soft pants in the background and then a scraping static from his speakers. He winced and turned down the volume.

"Dani, what's going on?" he asked, ready to whip around, one-way or not, and beat feet back the way they'd come.

"It's Steve. They messed him up pretty bad." There were tears in her voice. "I'm trying to make him comfortable until the ambulance arrives."

So much for holding her location.

"Be careful, you don't know if there are others," he warned. "Where's Cam?"

They heard the phone changing hands.

"Did you get a plate number?" Cam was all business.

Jason shared a raised eyebrow with his mother. She pursed her lips and shook her head, eyes worried.

Man, he hoped he wasn't making things worse with his decision to bring her along with him. The doctors had warned them to avoid stressful situations. He had a feeling this would count as one of those times.

"No, but I have a make and model, if that helps. Chev Impala, a '67, I believe. Navy blue, black roof."

There was a hesitation on the line. "Just how close are you, McIntyre?"

Jason grinned. "Close enough I can see the whites of his eyes, boss." Not quite, but it sounded good. "Is Steve going to make it? Ambulance should be there soon." The man had a kid, he'd better not die on them.

"It's here now, gotta go. Listen, do what you can, but keep it strictly surveillance. You got that? Stay safe, Jason."

Aw, he did care.

"Will do, boss. Keep me posted." He signed off and looked at his mom. "How are you doing? Is this too much for you? Tell me the truth, Mom. We can always quit and go for an ice cream."

She smiled. "Are you kidding? This is the most excitement I've had in… well, months. Lead on, maestro."

Relieved, Jason nodded and refocused on the car in front of them. It was moving toward his step-father's neighborhood, making it harder to follow without being made. What the hell was he doing here?

They were almost a block back now, so when the other car made a sharp left and disappeared it took precious seconds to gain the intersection. The car in front of him was toddling along like an old man with a walker. And since they were in residential, he had no way to get by him. Jason swore and tapped his horn, but if anything, it made the old guy move slower. They were going to lose their suspect if he didn't do something.

Checking there was no oncoming traffic, he dropped a gear and roared past the other car, taking the corner faster than was wise.

But they were too late, the Chev was gone.

Chapter Twenty-Nine

It wasn't often Tammy-Jo was able to spend time alone with her father. With her busy lifestyle, and his business interests combined with caring for Caroline, they rarely connected one on one. Which might be the reason she was having a hard time coming up with something to say that didn't sound like an accusation. There were too many coincidences for him not to at least have an idea of what was going on, and why anyone would want to kill Tim.

It had all clicked with the message on the card. Cards her husband had carried as general manager of

the country club. The same club her daddy had been a
member of for the past fifteen years.

"Dad…"

He looked up from gathering the last of the glass
and she hesitated, suddenly unsure of what to say. If
she was wrong it could seriously injure their
relationship. Then again, if she was right…

"Spit it out, girl," he said, turning away to dump
the dustpan.

She stared at his rounded shoulders and stooped
back. Where was the forceful presence of her youth?
The disease robbing Caroline of her dignity was also
taking a toll on him. She should have helped more,
alleviated some of the strain he'd been under. That
was her burden to bear.

"I could have visited more often," she said, and
shrugged uncomfortably under his regard. "You
should have called."

"And say what?" he asked, waving the empty
dustpan. Fragments of glass floated in the air creating
prisms of light as they drifted to the floor. "Caroline
bought ten quarts of milk today, need some? She

rearranged the cupboards and I found my socks beside the canned beets, isn't that a hoot?" He threw the dustpan aside and it clattered as it skidded across the tiles.

T.J. jumped. Her heart ached for the hopelessness and frustration stamped into the weary lines of his face. She was the most selfish daughter on the planet.

"I… I hadn't realized," she mumbled. He'd kept all of this from her until now. He must live in constant fear in case Caroline was cooking and walked away, starting a fire. And now she understood the need for the updated security system on the house—it was for his wife's safety.

He sighed, sat across from her, and rubbed the back of his neck before meeting her gaze. "She didn't want anyone to know, especially you and Jason. Her life is changing too fast as it is, she didn't want you kids acting different around her."

Tears blurred her father's dear face. "Daddy, I'm so sorry. Isn't there anything that can be done?"

He nodded. "There are studies in the U.K. and a couple of other countries, but they're far from ready for human trials. The only way is to jump the line and that takes money, a lot of money."

The numbers on those papers came back to haunt her. Had Tim been embezzling from the club to help her dad out? Was that what was going on? She needed to know the truth before she could find an answer. "Dad, are you in trouble?"

He looked away. "You mean other than old and tired? Of course not."

The response was too glib and they both knew it. He coughed, rose to walk over to the refrigerator, opened the door, and stared into the interior as though the solution was hiding behind the milk.

T.J. sighed. Maybe it was time to show him what she'd found.

"I'll be right back, Dad. I'll just run up and grab those papers we talked about." Hopefully then he would come clean and let her help him.

He turned around, a chocolate cake in his hands, a defensive look on his face. "Caroline made this for my birthday last week. I promised her I'd get it eaten. Hang on, I'll just set it down and come with you."

She waved him away. "No, cut us each a slice and I'll be back before you know it. I love Caroline's German chocolate cake." How had she missed his birthday? Some daughter she'd turned out to be. When this was over maybe they could have a father-daughter day, that is if Jason stayed long enough to keep his mother company.

Jason.

How was he going to feel about his mom's worsening condition? It was hard to imagine their lives without Caroline. She'd become the heart of their new family. They'd be lost without her.

The documents were right where she'd left them. Frankly, she would be relieved to get rid of them. The best thing she could do was call the police and turn the papers over, but not until her dad had a chance to explain.

The front door rattled just as T.J. was walking past and she hurried over, remembering she'd locked it earlier. Good, now Jason would be here too and they could sort this mess out together. She shut off the security system and turned the deadbolt, then tugged the door open. The welcoming smile on her lips turned questioning when she saw the elderly couple on the other side.

"Mr. and Mrs. Donaldson. This is a surprise." The two were long-standing board members of the Magnolia Country Club. She hadn't realized they were personal friends of her father's, too.

"Hello, my dear," Mrs. Donaldson answered, striding into the foyer ahead of her shorter husband, and forcing T.J. to take a step back. "We heard about the rather unfortunate circumstances surrounding Timothy's death and wanted to be the first to offer our condolences." She leaned forward and kissed the air beside Tammy-Jo's head before glancing around the entry. "Is your father home? As you might imagine, this has left the club in something of a quandary. We'd like to speak with him and get it sorted as soon as possible."

So much for their sympathy.

She nodded and waved a hand toward the kitchen. "You're just in time, we're about to have some birthday cake."

Mr. Donaldson's eyes lit up. "I never say no to cake. Talk about good timing."

Yeah. Never mind the fact T.J.'s husband was dead. She shook off the snide thought and followed the pair down the hall.

Her dad looked up with a mouthful of cake and almost dropped his fork. "What are you doing here?" he snapped, crumbs flying everywhere.

Mrs. Donaldson looked amused and disgusted in equal measure. "Is that any way to greet your guests, Samuel?" She folded her black leather driving gloves and set them on the table along with her clutch. "Is it your birthday, then? We're hurt you didn't invite us, aren't we, Sebastian?"

Mr. Donaldson grinned and helped himself to T.J.'s slice of cake sitting on the table. "And I thought we were friends," he murmured.

T.J. stared hard at her dad, trying to get his attention, but he was focused on the vipers she'd inadvertently let into the house. There were undercurrents flowing between the three of them she didn't understand, but it scared her that her father looked fearful.

Determined to gain the upper hand, she stepped forward and took the plate from Mr. Donaldson and pointed to the door. "I'm not sure what's going on, but this is a bad time. Can you leave, please? You can call my father in a few days, after the funeral."

Mrs. Donaldson smiled and took a seat. "She has spunk, Sam. Where have you been hiding her?"

He leaned forward and glared at the woman, his cheeks puffed and ruddy beneath his beard. "This is my *home*, Martha. We'll talk about whatever you want at the club. You have no business bringing it here."

She considered him for a long moment, then leaned back and laughed. "I'm impressed. You do have a backbone, I was beginning to wonder." She shared an amused glance with her husband. "There's hope for you yet, Sebastian."

His smile died.

"No need to be a hag, my beauty," he muttered.

T.J.'s dad rose from his chair and stalked across the room. "Enough. I want you gone before Caroline gets home."

Martha crossed her legs and set one foot to rocking. "Not so fast. We're tired of waiting, Sam. We want our merchandise, and we want it now." She fiddled with the clasp on her clutch, opened it, and withdrew a deadly-looking little black pistol.

Chapter Thirty

Tammy-Jo gasped and grabbed her daddy's arm, stopping his lunge toward the crazy woman sitting at their kitchen table with a gun in her hand.

A. Gun.

It was like some murder mystery she occasionally watched on the television. How had this become her life?

"Are you mad? The police will be here any minute." A false hope since she'd been stupid enough to let them into the house. "Why are you doing this?" Maybe her dad could give the Donaldsons what they wanted and they would consider not shooting them.

And as long as she was dreaming, maybe Caroline would be miraculously healed and Jason would show up, save the day, and declare his undying love and they'd all live happily ever after.

But this wasn't a movie, it was all too real, and she was petrified.

Her dad tried to shake loose of her grasp, stepping in front of her body to provide a shield, but T.J. wasn't having it. She clung like a limpet, scared he'd do something stupid and get himself shot.

"Let me handle this, daughter. It's my problem," he pleaded.

She shook her head and dug her hand into his jacket pocket, holding him in place. Her fingers connected with the hard case of his cell phone and hope soared. If she could just punch in the number for the police, help really would be on the way.

"Isn't that sweet," Martha cooed, her eyes narrowed as she watched them. "Daddy protecting his baby girl. Too bad he didn't think of that when he dragged your dumb-ass husband into his little scheme."

T.J. heard the faint voice of the emergency
responder coming from her dad's pocket at the same
time Mrs. Donaldson's words sank in. What did she
mean, *scheme*?

Oh Lord, Daddy, what did you do?

"I have no idea what you're talking about. Tim
was my father's partner. You must be confused.
Please put the *gun* down." She spoke loudly, doing
her best to muffle the operator while letting them
know the situation was dangerous.

"Oh, we know all about their so-called investor
group," Mr. Donaldson said. "We invested five
hundred thousand dollars with Hawthorne's guarantee
of a substantial return." He glanced at his wife. "You
can see how that worked out."

"Oh, my God. Did you kill Tim?" T.J. cried.

"No, they left that pleasure to me," a deep voice
growled from behind them.

Tammy-Jo jumped and swung around, heart
pounding. Her legs turned to jelly. It was the stranger
from the driveway, and his gun made Martha's look
like a kid's toy.

He smirked and snatched the papers she'd been holding behind her back. "Look what we have here." He waved them in the air. "I knew she had 'em."

"Give them to me, Leo," Martha demanded, eyes sparking with excitement. She unfolded from the chair, a cobra preparing to strike.

"Yeah, not so fast," he said, turning the gun on the other woman. "I've been thinking. It's time we come to a new set of terms."

Before T.J. knew what was happening, he'd grabbed her arm and yanked her away from her father, backing toward the hallway, his grip painfully strong.

"I'm tired of playing the game your way. Now I's got all the cards. You owe me, and I'm going to make sure you pay."

"Let go of my daughter, you... you simpleton," her dad demanded. He took a step forward, then stopped at her cry of anguish. The anger drained and desperation took its place. "Please. I'll give you whatever you want." His arm stretched out for her, pleading with her captor, but the man only laughed.

"Too little, too late. You rich snobs are alls alike. You think the world owes you them silver spoons ya eats with. Well, I have news for ya. We wipe our asses the same damn way." He gave T.J. a shake, rattling her teeth. "It's my turn to see how the other half lives. You have twenty-four hours to get me ten million, all in cash, or you won't see your pretty little gal alive again. Oh, and Mrs. D?" He stopped his backward momentum and T.J. held her breath, preparing for the fight of her life.

Martha hadn't flinched throughout the exchange. Her face was expressionless, except for those glittering green eyes. Even though Leo had the bigger gun, T.J. sensed where the real danger lay.

"Make it good, Leo. It might very well be your last request," she murmured. Sebastian grinned as though this was great entertainment.

T.J. felt hesitation run through Leo's body in the flexing of his fingers on her arm and the hitch in his breath. Smart man.

Until he opened his mouth.

"Before you threaten me," he said. "You might want to consider the fact these here papers are all the proof I need to go to the cops. You don't get me my money, I'll make sure all three of you spend the rest of your days in an eight-by-eight jail cell."

"If we go down, you'll go with us, and we aren't the ones who committed a murder." Martha's pointed chin rose. "Don't threaten me, Leo. You'll live to regret it."

"Shut up," T.J.'s dad snarled. "None of that matters. Nothing does except my daughter's safety." He turned to Leo, his gaze encouraging her to remain strong. "We'll do the best that we can…" he ignored Mrs. Donaldson's humph, "but ten million is a lot of money. You need to give us more time."

Leo's hold tightened, pinching the delicate skin of her underarm. T.J. let out a cry and tried again to tug herself free to no avail.

"You sonofabitch," her dad roared, lunging forward.

Everything happened in a horrifying blur after that. T.J. was shoved to the ground just as Leo turned the

gun on her father and pulled the trigger. She fell hard
on her wrist and felt as much as heard the snap. She
rolled, her back hitting the wall, and lay there for a
minute, breathing past the fear and the pain radiating
up through her arm.

The muffled thump of fist hitting flesh and male
grunts reached her first. Then the shuffle of boots
struggling for purchase on the hardwood floor. She
looked up to see Leo punch Jason in the ribs and use
his weight to shove him against the wall, rattling an
antique mirror hanging over her head. She screamed
and pitched forward, scrambling to get out of the
way.

The gun lay forgotten in the doorway to the
bathroom and she dove for it, cradling her injured
wrist as best she could. Dots swam in her vision, but
she managed to get her hand on the weapon. Once
more she rolled and lodged her back into the
doorjamb, resting the nose of the gun on her raised
knees.

"Freeze," she croaked, fear making her voice
husky. The men hesitated just long enough for Jason

to gain the upper hand. He slammed his fist into
Leo's face and blood spurted from the man's nose. He
howled and covered the injury, muddy brown eyes
watering from the pain. Jason swung him around and
twisted an arm up behind his back, holding him in
place.

"You okay?" he said, glancing over his shoulder.

She started to nod, then saw his attention slide past
her to the kitchen. She turned her head, afraid of what
she would see.

Caroline had entered by the back door and stood,
phone in hand, staring at the gun Martha had trained
on T.J.'s father.

Oh no.

"Caro," her dad said, his voice shaky. "I think I
forgot my briefcase in the garage. Be a doll and grab
it for me, will you?"

Caroline hesitated, her brow furrowing as she
looked from him to the Donaldsons. Then she moved
determinedly forward and set the phone on the
counter near the sink. Martha followed her with her
eyes but kept the gun steady on T.J.'s dad.

She turned, a vacant smile on her face that made Martha relax and everyone else tense. "Martha, Sebastian, how exciting. It's been such a long while since we've visited."

Sebastian gazed at her, his face filled with cynicism. "An hour or two, anyway."

Martha shushed him. "Don't be rude, darling. It's not Caroline's fault that she gets confused." She nodded toward the table. "Have a seat, you look rather tired, my dear. We have some business to attend to with Samuel and then we'll get out of your hair."

T.J. held her breath and prayed Jason's mom would do as she was told. But of course she was as stubborn as her son.

"I could use a cup of tea. Would you and Sebastian like to join me?" She turned away and flipped on the tap, her voice rising above the flow of water. "I've found the nicest blend of jasmine tea, it helps me sleep at night. You just have to try it."

On the final word, she swung around, the commercial style sink nozzle in hand, and sprayed

steaming hot water across the kitchen, catching
Martha and her husband completely by surprise.

Tammy-Jo would have laughed at the stunned look
on their dripping wet faces if not for the dangerous
situation. The gun wavered in the older woman's
hand and T.J. quickly raised her own weapon, hoping
they wouldn't realize she had no idea how to use it.

"Drop the gun," she yelled, and this time her voice
had enough conviction behind it, Martha listened.

Her dad hurried forward, his gait awkward, and
took the pistol out of the woman's lax hand.

Caroline rushed to his side. "You're hurt," she
cried.

He kissed her forehead. "It's just a scratch, thanks
to you." He waved the firearm toward the far corner
of the room, well away from anything they could use
as weapons. "Move it," he said.

Just then they heard the wail of sirens pulling up to
the house and this time when Caroline smiled it was
filled with tenderness. "About time they got here. I
had the phone on speaker the whole time."

Tammy-Jo breathed a sigh of relief and turned her head to meet Jason's warm blue gaze. They were going to be okay.

Epilogue

It was family day at the Magnolia General Hospital. Jason had been making the rounds all morning. He'd spent a long night with his mother in the waiting room while the doctors operated to reset and pin Tammy-Jo's fractured wrist, stitch up her father's side where the bullet from Leo's gun had grazed him, and run a series of x-rays on Steve's hard head before binding his badly bruised ribs and giving everyone the all-clear to leave.

The SEC and local police were finally working together. They'd arrived at the Millar house in time to make their arrests of the Donaldsons, and Leo, who was singing like a jay bird. They hadn't tracked down all the money yet, but it was just a matter of time. It seemed Sam had started the investors group with the goal of gathering enough funds to seek a cure for the disease destroying his wife's mind and body. Jason couldn't fault the man for that. The trouble started when he allowed the Donaldsons in with their connections to the mob. Apparently, Tim had been trying to play both ends against the middle and paid the ultimate price for his greed.

Jason stood near the entrance doors with his team and watched Sam and his mother greet T.J. when she was wheeled into the waiting room by a perky hospital attendant. He ached to be with them, wrapped in the cocoon of love encircling his family like an aura, but he was the outsider—the man responsible for the cuffs holding Sam's arms behind his back.

"How long do you think he'll go down for?" he asked Cam.

His friend patted his back. "Not long. He was as much victim as perpetrator. I think when the courts hear his plea they'll cut him a deal. As long as he leads them to the cash, of course." He grinned. "Now your mom on the other hand, if she ever needs a job tell her to look us up. She was brilliant yesterday. That'll be a story for the logbooks."

Warmth filled Jason's chest. He'd been scared shitless when she appeared in the house—after he'd expressly told her to remain in the car—but there was no denying she'd saved them all from what could have been serious injury. He was damn proud of her.

"How come I didn't get a nurse like that?" Steve grumbled, his gaze woebegone in a scraped and bruised face. A light gauze covered his head where the doctor had shaved his hair to stitch the three-inch gash along his temple and supportive bandages circled his ribs. Jason could tell it cost him to talk. Poor Dodger, with his blackbelt in Taekwondo, it wasn't often anyone got the drop on him. His confidence had taken a beating along with his body.

"You're too butt ugly for the likes of her," Jason joked. "Better wait until you lose the shiner before you ask a woman out, or they'll run in the other direction."

Dani gave him a hard nudge with her elbow. "Ignore Boy Wonder, here, Steve. He's just jealous 'cause you can get a date and he can't on account of him being in *lurve* and all." The words were filled with sarcasm, but her smile was wistful as it settled on Cam.

Jason wasn't much of a matchmaker, but if those two didn't get things figured out soon he was going to throw them in a room together and lock the door.

She was right about one thing though, he loved Tammy-Jo Hawthorne, and it was time she knew it. He couldn't blame her if she never forgave him his part in having her father arrested. But he needed her to know how he felt. How he'd always felt.

"Tammy-Jo," he called, startling the busy doctors and nurses hurrying through the lobby. A young couple with a fretful baby in the waiting room glanced around, and two patrolmen keeping watch over Sam straightened, their disinterested gazes turning sharp and focused.

Nothing like a public declaration to make a guy
sweat.

Gathering his courage, he walked across the
distance separating him from his family. His mother
gave him an encouraging smile, Sam nodded, as
though he approved of what was to come, and T.J....
she waited.

"Mind if I have a word with you?" he asked, angry
with himself for not making a move on Leo before
she got hurt. He'd driven the damn neighborhood for
half an hour or more looking for the Chevy before
admitting defeat and driving his mom home, only to
see the car parked down the road from their house.
His heart had literally stopped. By the time he
managed to sneak into the foyer, leaving his mom to
watch for the police, it had almost been too late. He
shuddered, the memory of T.J. in that man's grasp
and the gun he'd been holding still enough to turn his
stomach inside out with fear.

"There's nothing you can say that my father can't
hear," she said, her voice stiff. "No more secrets. I
think we've had enough revelations, don't you?"

Hopefully, she would accept one more.

His palms were sweaty and he rubbed them on his jeans before sinking to one knee, right there in the middle of Magnolia General, and God, and everybody.

"Tammy-Jo Hawthorne, I love you." He took encouragement from her startled gasp. "I've been a stupid idiot for far too long, but I'm ready to change." He pleaded with her to understand. "When I left Magnolia all those years ago, it was for the best." He glanced at Sam, surprised to see tears standing in the man's eyes. "I had too much anger and attitude to appreciate what we had together. Eventually, it would have destroyed us."

He reached out and grasped her shaking fingers, his own none too steady as he slid the diamond ring he'd bought for her at eighteen onto her hand. It was nowhere near the size of the one that had rested there previously, but it was precious to him and he hoped she would understand the significance.

She raised tear-stained eyes to his, her mouth wobbling as she gazed at him in wonder. "Is this…?"

He breathed a sigh of relief. She did remember.

"Uh, huh. It's the ring you had your eye on before graduation. You must have showed it to me ten times or more." He laughed, his throat choked with emotion. "I planned to give it to you at prom, but…" He shrugged, unwilling to ruin the moment.

"But I threatened you and sent you packing," Sam said. "Good lord, you must hate me." His shoulders bowed and he shook his head. "I'm so sorry, son. So very sorry."

Jason swallowed hard, touched by this man who'd been his nemesis for half his life. Maybe they had a chance after all.

But it was up to T.J.

He turned to her and was overwhelmed by the love swimming in those beautiful tawny eyes.

"It's about time," she whispered. "Let's go home."

A Note From The Author

This story is special for me. A few years ago my grandmother was diagnosed with dementia. At the time, we put her change in demeanor and forgetfulness down to old age. It took a medical emergency before we found out the truth.

She's been gone ten years now and I still miss her every day.

Other Books by This Author

Wounded Hearts Series

Tidal Falls

The Rebel's Redemption

Twilight's Encore

The Sheriff Meets His Match

Summer Lovin'

Wounded Hearts Box Set

Coming Soon- Maggie's Revenge

Mended Souls Series

The Guardian

The Beast Within

Single Titles

Silver Bells

Missing: The Lady Said No

Hold 'Em

My Baby Wrote Me A Letter

Tempted by Mr. Wrong

About the Author

JACQUIE BIGGAR is a USA Today bestselling author of Romantic Suspense who loves to write about tough, alpha males and strong, contemporary women willing to show their men that true power comes from love.

She is the author of the popular Wounded Hearts series and has just started a new series in paranormal suspense, Mended Souls.

She has been blessed with a long, happy marriage and enjoys writing romance novels that end with happily-ever-afters.

Jacquie lives in paradise along the west coast of Canada with her family and loves reading, writing, and flower gardening. She swears she can't function without coffee, preferably at the beach with her sweetheart. :)

Free reads, excerpts, author news, and contests can be found on her web site:

http://jacqbiggar.com

You can follow her on at

http://Facebook.com/jacqbiggar,

http://Twitter.com/jacqbiggar

Or email her via her web site. Jacquie lives on Vancouver Island with her husband and loves to hear from readers all over the world!

You can also join her street team on Facebook:

Biggar's Book Buddies

Or her exclusive Review Crew:

https://jacqbiggar.com/join-my-review-crew/

And sign up for her newsletter-

https://app.mailerlite.com/webforms/landing/h6c2n8